CONTENTS

DIANA JFEBRY

TROUBLE AT CROWCOMBE

By Diana J Febry

COVER IMAGE - BIGSTOCK
COVER DESIGN – DIANA J FEBRY
Proofreader - @proofersj

CHAPTER ONE

Charlie Hobson smiled at his suitcase, stood neatly in the hall, locked his flat door, and crossed the yard to the farmhouse. The spring sunshine promised warmth later, but he quickened his pace in the fresh, early morning chill. He was cautiously optimistic that Simon would have thought over his comments from last night and come around to his way of thinking.

He wouldn't have taken the case if Peter hadn't agreed to lead the investigation in his absence. He had expected some resistance from Simon when he told him, but not at the level of the outburst of indignation last night. Charlie had put it down to the amount of wine he had drunk, something he was doing a lot recently.

Any idiot could see something was bothering Simon, but as he wouldn't say what it was, Charlie was rapidly running out of patience. For the hundredth time, he wondered how Kate put up with his mood swings.

Simon always used to be good-natured and laidback, so his violent opposition to Peter had shaken Charlie. Never a great fan of confrontation, he had left early and gone home to a restless night's sleep. He had only fallen asleep when he convinced himself that Simon would return to his affable self once he sobered up and agreed to Peter's involvement. As the front door loomed closer, he questioned whether he was kidding himself.

Peter could handle the case unassisted, if necessary, but he'd had his own problems recently. Worst case scenario, he could tell Lucy there would be a delay in the investigation until he returned home if Simon's attitude hadn't changed. Either way, it needed to be resolved before he left. He crossed his fingers and knocked on the door. Out of habit or possibly to delay things, he took his time to wipe his feet on the mat when Kate called out, "Come in. It's unlocked."

Charlie readied himself for the onslaught of the dogs and pushed the door open. As the dogs skidded around the corner, the usual scrabble of paws was followed by them pelting along the corridor towards him at full speed. Charlie had never considered himself to be a dog person, but their exuberant greeting always lightened his heart and made him smile. He braced himself for the onslaught and pushed his way through, patting Albert and Alfred before turning his attention to his secret favourite, Popeye. She immediately rolled onto her back for a belly scratch as the other two rushed back to the kitchen to check they hadn't missed any food falling from the table.

Popeye, the strange little terrier-type dog that Kate had found and nursed back to health, trotted alongside Charlie as he walked to the kitchen. He liked to think the sensitive little dear was giving him her moral support. Albert and Alfred were under the table, sat to attention intently watching Simon eat a piece of toast. Popeye left Charlie's side to jump onto her bed and looked adoringly at Kate.

"Morning," Charlie said, unsure of the reception he would receive from Simon.

"Sit down," Kate said. Leaning against the counter, she gave him a welcoming smile. "Coffee is on its way. Do you want anything else? I'm making scrambled eggs. Do you want some?"

"Just a coffee, please." Rubbing his stomach, Charlie said, "You're already responsible for most of this."

"Get away with you." Kate placed a coffee mug in front of Charlie and crossed the kitchen to pour scrambled eggs over two plates of toast for herself and Simon. Returning to the table with the plates, she said, "You're a fine figure of a man. You'll be fighting off all the single women on your trip. Are you sure you don't want anything to eat?"

"I've already eaten," Charlie lied. It smelled delicious, but Simon wasn't the only reason for his broken sleep. His stomach was already churning at the prospect of his flight to Malta. He hadn't admitted to anyone that it would be his first flight and he was secretly petrified.

Concentrating on covering his eggs with brown sauce, Simon said, "Kate is worried you're going to meet the woman of your dreams and sail away into the sunset, never to return."

"No, I'm not," Kate said, punching Simon. "It would be lovely if Charlie was to meet someone."

"Hello. Charlie is here and isn't planning on meeting anyone," he said. Glancing across at Simon, he couldn't tell whether he remembered last night's heated discussion.

"If you say so," Simon said, tucking into his breakfast.

"You'll have a lovely, relaxing time away from us," Kate said.

"Are you still okay to drive me to the airport?" Charlie asked, trying to work out if Simon was giving him the cold shoulder.

"Of course," Kate said. "Bring your suitcase over any time after eleven, and we'll set off shortly after. I checked your flight first thing this morning. It's due to leave on time."

"Thanks," Charlie said, savouring his coffee. Kate made everything taste delicious as easily as she made the draughty old farmhouse warm and cosy, and him welcome and at ease. Sometimes, Simon didn't know how lucky he was. He risked another glance at Simon, sneaking bits of toast under the table to the two eager dogs, still unsure if he was in his bad books.

Simon drank some coffee and cleared his throat, although he didn't look up to make eye contact. "About last night. I've spoken to Kate and had the chance to think about the case. I reckon I could learn a few things from this Peter Hatherall fellow if he's as experienced as you say. It makes sense to have an ex-copper onboard if we're questioning a police investigation."

"My friend, Fiona, says he's the best and he taught her everything she knows," Kate chipped in.

Charlie mouthed a thank you to Kate and said, "Well, if you're happy, the meeting is still arranged."

Making a fuss of his two dogs under the table, Simon said, "I suppose we had better get going soon."

"Finish your breakfast first," Charlie said. "I'm going in early to make sure the paperwork is all up to date."

Simon gave the crusts of his toast to the dogs. "I won't be long behind you."

After collecting the plates from the table, Kate said, "I'll be around some of the time to help if needed, but I'll be away for a few days this week on a house-sitting job. Someone was let down at the last minute, and I couldn't say no."

"Okay, thanks for the coffee," Charlie said, hiding his disappointment. Simon was more reliable when Kate was around, but she had her own work commitments. He got up and carried his empty mug to the counter. On his way out, he said to Simon, "I'll see you in the office."

After saying goodbye to Charlie, Kate joined Simon at the table. "Are you really okay about things? That was quite a turnaround. Last night, you were adamant you didn't want Peter babysitting you."

"I figured I don't have a choice, so I might as well approach the matter optimistically with an open mind. That's what all your magazines say to do, isn't it? It might make a pleasant change to work with someone else."

Sounding doubtful, Kate said, "That's great if you're sure. It's just … well…you've been a bit up and down recently."

"Have I? That's normal, isn't it?" Simon laughed. "A little bit high, a little bit low." He stood and gave his dogs a last pat. "I'll tell you all about it when I get back."

"I look forward to it." After Simon left, Kate's smile turned to a frown. Something wasn't right with Simon. She could only hope he would tell her what was bothering him in his own time.

CHAPTER TWO

Peter Hatherall checked his appearance in the hallway mirror before picking up his car keys. Surprised by his nerves, he wiped his sweaty palms on his jeans. When Charlie first approached him, the idea of helping on the occasional private investigation seemed perfect for him. He had years of experience with the police and was never happier than when he had a complex mystery to dissect. During the last few days, doubts had started to creep in. With the police, there was structure and an entire team of experts working behind the scenes. He may not have always liked the rules and procedures, but he understood them, and while he didn't slavishly follow them, they provided a recognisable framework.

He had only met Simon in passing, and Charlie's description of his work ethic didn't fill him with confidence. Was he ready to go it alone with only the assistance of an impetuous dreamer? Fiona had pointed him out a couple of times in the past, usually when they were in the pub, but he hadn't taken any notice other than to register that he looked very comfortable propping up a bar. With the occasional exception of Humphries, he was used to working alongside a team of disciplined, trained officers.

As a DCI he was also used to having the final say on operational matters and the authority of rank over junior officers. Although Charlie wanted him to lead the investigation, Simon co-owned the business, so while less experienced he would be his employer. He took a last look in the mirror, threw his keys in the air, caught them, and told himself to get a grip. He would work it out.

Driving to meet Simon and Charlie, he turned up the radio to blank out the occasional resurfacing of doubts. He had a rough outline of the case, but Charlie had said he wanted them to meet Lucy Lewis with open minds before they read through his notes. All he knew was her father had been charged with the murder of her stepmother, and she wanted them to prove he wasn't responsible. Charlie thought the police had been too quick to make assumptions and much of the evidence was circumstantial. He had mentioned the name of the DI who had directly handled the case. Peter had been tempted to call him yesterday for some background information but decided to wait until he had met the daughter, as Charlie wanted.

A waft of fresh coffee hit Peter as he opened the office door to the agency. Charlie greeted him warmly and led him through the reception area, which was spacious and inviting, into a back room where they clearly did most of their work. Simon jumped up energetically to shake hands. On first impressions, Peter wouldn't have thought him lazy. If anything, Simon had too much nervous energy as he grasped his hand firmly and shook it vigorously. He was blond and good-looking, with an open face and intelligent, sharp eyes.

"Hi, I'm pleased to meet you," Simon said, finally releasing Peter's hand. "Charlie has told me all about you. I'm looking forward to us working together."

Charlie handed Peter a coffee and sat. "Lucy will be here in about fifteen minutes. Like I said over the phone, I want you both to listen to her without any preconceived ideas, as I did. She has no doubts about her father's innocence."

"Did you have any doubts when you first spoke to her?" Peter asked.

Charlie smiled and drank his coffee. "I'll tell you later. Meanwhile, before I forget," he said, opening a desk drawer. "Here's a set of office keys, your official ID card and business cards. I'll explain the alarm system to you before I leave."

"I can do that," Simon offered enthusiastically.

Charlie nodded his thanks and continued, "Work from here, from home or wherever suits you two best. You'll find a copy of the police report on the computer, including all the statements they collected. You might be able to get hold of some additional information that didn't make the official report from the officers, if you know them."

"It would be great to have some additional insight," Simon said.

"I'll do my best," Peter said, wondering if Simon always sounded so enthusiastic. The way he bounced around the office was akin to a pea on a drum.

"I made some notes of the people I wanted to speak to and how I would approach the case. It's all in the file for reference, but I'll leave you to make your own decisions," Charlie said.

"Have you spoken to her father?" Peter asked.

"His name is Rob Lewis, but no. I thought I would leave that to you," Charlie said. "I've made an appointment for you to visit him this afternoon where he's being held on remand. It'll give you enough time to familiarize yourselves with the file and each other before meeting him."

Peter started to ask why Rob was being held on remand, but Simon spoke over him. "An organised trip to the local prison while you're landing in Malta for a week of wine, women and song. I know which I think sounds more fun."

"Sadly, not everything in this life is fun," Charlie replied. "If Rob is found guilty, he faces a long jail sentence."

"You still haven't said why you think he's innocent," Simon said.

"Because I want you to make your own minds up," Charlie said, before jumping up from his chair. "That sounds like Lucy arriving. She's early."

Simon and Peter shared a look, sizing each other up as they followed Charlie out to the reception area to greet Lucy.

CHAPTER THREE

Lucy Lewis shuffled in behind Charlie, looking at the floor. She was slight with a look of vulnerability and in her early to mid-twenties. Her straight, dark blonde hair was held back in a ponytail, and she was casually dressed in a white shirt, a black pinafore dress and Doc Martens carrying a heavy hessian bag. When she raised her head, her shy, guarded smile turned her pretty face into a stunning one.

There was sadness lurking behind her blue eyes, and Peter instantly felt drawn to her. He wanted to know more about her and her past, even protect her. He noticed Simon was equally struck by her. He looked closer at Lucy, questioning whether she was aware of her allure and whether it was natural or fake.

"Come and sit down," Charlie said. "These are my colleagues Simon Morris and Peter Hatherall. They will be working on your father's case while I'm away. I would like you to tell them what you told me, but first, can I get you a drink?"

Lucy pulled a water bottle from her bag. In a quiet voice with a slight lisp that added to her charm, she asked, "Could you refill this, please?"

Taking the water bottle, Charlie said, "Can you lock the door and draw the blinds, Simon? I think it will be more comfortable if the four of us stay here rather than squeeze into the back room, and I don't want us to be interrupted."

Simon leapt up with a foolish grin, almost falling over his feet in his dash to please.

Once Charlie had returned with the water bottle and they were seated, Lucy took a deep breath and said, "My father has been wrongly charged with the murder of his girlfriend Jane, who I viewed as my stepmother, and I want you to prove his innocence."

"Don't be nervous," Charlie said in a soothing voice. "Take your time to tell us what happened that evening."

Still rushing through her words, Lucy said, "Jane Forbes was killed in her home ... our home on a Friday night. I had seen her earlier in the evening between returning from work and going to stay with my boyfriend, as I do most weekends. After packing my bag, we had a quick chat in the kitchen, and Jane said Dad was taking her out for a meal later."

"Was your dad at home, then?" Simon asked.

"No, he was still at work," Lucy said.

"Maybe we could leave questions until the end," Charlie said. "For now, let's let Lucy tell us what happened. You will both have plenty of time for questions at the end."

Lucy gave Charlie a small smile. "There's not much more to say. The police came to my boyfriend's home the following morning to say Jane had been murdered. They asked us lots of questions about where we were and left. A week or so later, they arrested my father. I thought they would quickly release him when they realised that he was innocent. Instead of properly investigating the murder, they are focused on twisting the facts to make him look guilty, which is a mistake. Dad didn't kill Jane. He's not capable of killing anyone. Meanwhile, the real killer is walking around out there. For all I know, I could have passed him in the street today. I want you to prove he's an innocent man and the police are wrong."

CHAPTER FOUR

Peter waited to be sure Lucy had finished and looked at Charlie before asking, "Have the police told you they've completed their investigations?"

"They won't tell me anything, but it's obvious they are scratching around trying to find evidence to prove my dad's guilt instead of looking for anyone else in connection to the murder. Holding him on remand is completely unfair when he's innocent," Lucy said. "I have nightmares every night about them trying to beat a false confession from him."

Thinking the police must be confident of having the correct man, Peter asked, "Why are the police so sure your father was responsible?"

Looking down, Lucy said, "Because they're putting two and two together and coming up with five."

"If we're going to help your father, we need to know all the details," Peter said. "The police must have reasonable grounds for holding him."

"If only so we can prove them unfounded," Simon chipped in.

Lucy sighed, and said, "Dad had argued with Jane earlier in the evening after I left. The next-door neighbour heard shouting and what sounded like things being thrown around. There's evidence that Jane scratched Dad's face." Lucy clenched her teeth and looked up. "But that doesn't mean anything. Dad would never hit a woman, let alone stab Jane to death. He adored her."

"Did they go out for the meal?" Peter asked.

Lucy shook her head. "Apparently not. After they argued, Dad stormed off alone to the nearest pub. It's clear to everyone who knows Dad that someone came to the house after he left and stabbed Jane with a knife taken from the kitchen drawer. It's only the stupid police who think it was Dad."

"Was the knife left at the scene?" Peter asked.

"I guess. They showed me a picture of a knife, and I said it looked like one from Jane's set. When they made me check, I saw that one was missing. I asked them if they had fingerprint evidence, but they wouldn't say. What would it prove anyway? Dad's fingerprints will be all over the house."

"Did they ask you for your fingerprints?" Peter asked.

"Yes, for elimination or something."

"Are there witnesses to your dad being in the pub?" Simon asked.

"Yes, several," Lucy said. "He stayed at a friend's house that night, and Duncan, that's the friend who put him up for the night, has said that Dad could barely stand, let alone kill anyone."

"Do you know what time Jane was attacked?" Peter asked.

"They say between eight o'clock that night and one o'clock the following morning," Lucy said.

Simon frowned. "When was your dad in the pub with his mate?"

Lucy shrugged. "He arrived shortly after eight. There were people in the pub who knew him, but he was drinking alone. He walked to a park bench when he was thrown out at closing time. He woke up sometime later, feeling sick and cold, so he staggered to Duncan's house and banged on the door to be let in. And no, he wasn't covered in blood. Duncan said he fell in through the door when he opened it and bumped into several walls before collapsing on the sofa. If he had just stabbed someone, wouldn't there have been smears of blood all over the wall? There wasn't, by the way. Duncan told me they checked."

"What time did he arrive at his friend's house?" Simon asked.

"Duncan can't be sure, but he thinks it was around one o'clock. He threw a blanket over Dad and went back to bed."

Duncan was high on Peter's list of people he wanted to see. Bleary-eyed from being woken up, he could easily have missed small stains if Rob had stopped to clean himself up. He also couldn't be sure of the time. It could have been much later. "Did the police ask Duncan if he thought your dad had recently showered?"

"I don't know. You'll have to ask him, but he told me Dad stunk of booze."

"Were any items of blood-stained clothing found?"

"Yes, but only from when Dad found Jane in the morning," Lucy said.

"It was your father who found Jane and raised the alarm?" Peter asked.

"Yes, the following morning, once he sobered up, he bought a bunch of flowers from the local garage and walked home. He found Jane in the living room. Once he had checked whether she was alive or not, he called the police, so of course, he was covered in her blood when they arrived."

Peter turned to Charlie. "Is there a forensic report on Rob's clothing in the official report?"

Charlie nodded. "It was one of the first things I looked for. The report is inconclusive."

"How long has your dad been in a relationship with Jane?" Peter asked.

"Nearly five years. Before that, it was only the two of us," Lucy said.

"And how long have you been seeing your boyfriend?" Simon asked.

"Umm, not so long. Maybe a year."

Peter shot Simon a sideways glance before asking, "Was Rob a good father?"

"The best. I've never had any reason to be afraid of him, if that's what you mean. He was stricter than you might expect about certain things, but he's never raised a hand to me."

"Are you close?"

Lucy nodded. "When I was little, he was always there for me and made me feel safe. As I grew older, we've always talked things out. I grew up feeling I could turn to him about anything.

Nothing was off limits. If I needed to talk about things, he was there to listen. You must believe me when I say he couldn't kill anyone. He hasn't got it in him."

"He sounds like a great father," Simon said.

"What sort of things was he strict about?" Peter asked.

"Respect. He's big on respect. Respecting yourself and others. He likes good manners, and he has principles. One of which was you don't hit women or anyone or anything weaker than yourself. He believed in holding doors open, saying please and thank you. That sort of stuff."

"How does he get along with your mother?" Peter asked.

Lucy fell silent and took a sip of her water. She screwed the lid back on and carefully placed the bottle on the table. "My mother was killed in a hit-and-run accident when I was five. They never did find the driver. Dad was devastated. He didn't date or anything when I was younger. He gave up everything to care for me. Like I said, we're close. For Dad's sake, you need to discover who killed Jane. He can't go through it all again."

"Through what again?" Peter asked.

"Everything. This," Lucy said, looking flustered.

"Was the hit-and-run local?" Peter asked.

"It was in Cuxwold, not far from the main shopping centre."

"About twenty years ago?" Peter asked, thinking he had no idea where Cuxwold was, but he needed to see a copy of that accident report.

"About that, yes," Lucy said. "I don't remember anything about it, but I believe it was in the news at the time. There were several witnesses, and they even had the sense to take the car registration number. Not that it helped, as the plates were fake. The car was found burnt out several miles away."

"It's terrible that your father has lost two partners in violent situations," Simon said.

Peter thought, 'Isn't it just,' but said nothing. Instead, he asked, "Where did your father and Jane live?"

"Crowcombe," Lucy said. "We gave up our flat and moved in with Jane a couple of years ago."

"That's some distance from here," Peter said. "Why haven't you contacted a more local firm of investigators?"

"It's likely the case will be heard in Birstall, so I thought a firm from somewhere in between would work best. I stuck a pin in the map, and here we are."

As everyone fell silent, Charlie said, "Peter and Simon have the police files to read through, and then they'll discuss where to go from here. Is there anything else you can tell them that might help?"

"Not really, other than my dad would never hurt Jane. Sure, they argued, but it was never physical, and they always made up afterwards. He is innocent."

"Where are you staying at the moment?" Peter asked.

"With my boyfriend, for now, a few miles from Crowcombe. I gave Charlie my contact details," Lucy said. "Do you want them again?"

"That's fine. They'll be on file," Peter said.

"Do you have any family you could stay with?" Simon asked.

"Dad was an only child. His parents were great and helped out when I was younger, but they're long gone," Lucy said. "Jane had a brother, but he has always given me the creeps. Jane used to make excuses for him, but he's a jerk. He never cared too much about her wellbeing before, but he's making out he's devastated by her death. I'm sure he pushed for Dad's arrest, and then he had the nerve to try to be friendly with me. I would die before I moved in with him. It wouldn't surprise me if he had something to do with the attack."

"Why do you say that?" Peter asked.

"He's horrible, and he was always hassling Jane for money."

"Does this brother have a name? And where does he live?" Peter asked.

"Chris Forbes, but I haven't a clue where he lives."

"Do you have any friends you could stay with?" Simon suggested.

"There's no need. I'm happy where I am, and it's only temporary until Dad is released. We'll be fine - just like we were before," Lucy said. "You need to make the police hurry up and see sense."

"We'll do our best," Simon said. "We're seeing your dad this afternoon, and I'm sure we'll get to the bottom of it."

Peter watched the smile Lucy gave Simon, and how it affected him. He only knew of Simon's partner as Fiona's friend, but he didn't think she would be too happy with the way he looked at Lucy. Not that it was his concern.

Lucy was an intriguing girl, and he could see the attraction, but listening to her account, his suspicion that the air of frailty was an act and underneath was something much tougher had increased. Her relationship with her father seemed incredibly close. He had brought up Amelia as a single father in similar circumstances, and while they got along well now, her transition to adulthood had been fraught with arguments, and she had objected to every one of his girlfriends.

"Peter?"

Charlie's voice cut through Peter's thoughts, and he quickly shook Lucy's hand as she prepared to leave. "Once I've read the police report and spoken to a few people, I'll give you an honest assessment."

Lucy held onto his hand longer than necessary, saying, "You'll realise my dad is innocent and prove it, I'm sure." She was smiling, but her eyes said, 'You had better.'

CHAPTER FIVE

After seeing Lucy out, Charlie led Peter and Simon to the back room. Sitting, he asked, "What do you think?"

"She's a lovely girl, and I'm sure we can help her," Simon said. "Coffees all round?"

While Simon disappeared into the small kitchen at the rear and busied himself with the coffee machine, Peter said, "I have some reservations, but I'll keep an open mind until I've read the file and spoken to a few people. What time are we booked in to see Rob?"

"Two o'clock," Charlie said. "Initial thoughts?"

"The argument and the unaccounted hours on a street bench concern me," Peter said.

"We should be able to find witnesses to how drunk he was in the pub, and we might find someone who saw him sleeping it off on the bench," Simon said, emerging from the kitchen and handing out the coffees.

"True," Peter said. "I want a copy of the report on his first wife's death, and Lucy's animosity towards Jane's brother is interesting. Chris might have a different opinion on his sister's relationship with Rob. There could be a history of abuse despite what Lucy said. To my mind, losing two wives to violence is more than unlucky."

"I admit that was news to me," Charlie said.

"Potentially, it could dramatically change things, especially if there was any suggestion Rob may have had a hand in his first wife's death," Peter said. "What about the daughter?"

"I thought she was very level-headed," Simon said. "She's convinced her dad is innocent and she would know him better than anyone. Living in the same house, she's in a far better position than Jane's brother to judge the relationship."

"Do we know how she got along with Jane? She didn't strike me as someone in mourning, and she likes the idea of it being just her and her dad," Peter said.

"What! You can't be serious," Simon said, twigging Peter's line of thought.

"Keeping an open mind means everyone is a suspect," Peter said. "She had the opportunity and possibly motive."

"She was at her boyfriend's house and thought her dad was taking Jane out for a meal that night," Simon protested.

"According to her," Peter said. "We won't know for sure until we've spoken to her father and boyfriend."

"It needs checking, but I think you'll find she's telling the truth," Charlie said. "I take your point about her not appearing upset, but she's had time to get over the shock, and I didn't detect any animosity between her and Jane. When you read the statements, you'll see that Rob was planning to take Jane out for a meal. You can ask him how the two women got along when you meet him."

"Why didn't they go out for the meal?" Simon asked.

Charlie looked at the time and finished his coffee. "It's all in the report, and I have a plane to catch."

"We can always call you if something comes up," Simon said.

Charlie stood. "Only if it's something you can't answer yourself."

"Fair enough," Peter said. He stood to shake Charlie's hand. "Have a great holiday."

"Have fun," Simon said. "I'm sure Kate will have lots of advice for you, from applying sufficient sun cream to handling a holiday romance. Don't worry about anything here. We have it all in hand, and we'll see you next week."

Once Charlie was gone, Peter said, "Time to make a start on reading the file and then we can swap notes before we visit Rob."

"Works for me," Simon said, looking down at his phone. "It will take about twenty minutes to drive to where they are holding

Rob, so we should give ourselves half an hour. If we stop at twelve, we'll have time to grab lunch and chat about plans over a beer before we speak to Rob. What do you think?"

"It will have to be soft drinks," Peter said. As a concession, he suggested they discuss the case over a pint at the end of the day.

"Okay. The Shipp opens at five, and the Royal Oak is open all day. They both serve a decent pint. You can choose," Simon said. "Have you brought your own laptop? I'll email the files over to you."

"Thanks," Peter said, ducking under the table to pull his laptop from his backpack. "While you do that, I'll see if I can get hold of the report on the death of his first wife."

"You might need our code," Simon said, walking to Charlie's desk. "Charlie keeps it in here somewhere. Ah, here it is. Put this at the top of the online request."

Peter took the sheet of paper, placed it next to his laptop and picked up his phone. "I'll try the personal touch first." He ended his call with a smile. "We should have the report in a couple of hours."

Simon nodded an acknowledgement, and Peter settled down to open his laptop. He started with the murder scene report. The attack had taken place in the living room and had been vicious and erratic. He scrolled through the pages and noted over twenty distinct stab wounds were recorded. The assailant would have been covered in blood. Rob's friend would have noticed unless Rob had a complete change of clothes and a shower, even if he was half asleep.

Peter scrolled back through the report. There was no sign of a forced entry, so it was likely that Jane had let her killer into the house. Living room, kitchen and bedroom drawers had been pulled out and presumably searched before being thrown to the floor, but no valuables had been taken. Someone who knew Jane and was looking for something specific they thought was kept in the house? Or someone trying to make it look like a burglary that had gone wrong?

"You don't really think Lucy could be responsible, do you?"

Simon asked.

"We can't discount it yet," Peter replied without looking up and carried on reading.

A few minutes later, Peter glanced across at Simon, who was looking at the ceiling, either thinking or daydreaming. Peter suspected the latter and returned his attention to the file. Jane had been wearing pyjamas and a dressing gown. Had she already gone to bed, or was she snuggled down for a night in? Either way, she wasn't dressed to go out for dinner or to receive an expected visitor.

He flicked to the statement of the officers first on the scene. Rob had been found kneeling next to Jane, cradling her. The officer noted there was a strong smell of alcohol on his breath, and he was crying. Peter read the inconclusive report on his clothing. Not surprisingly, they had found plenty of blood stains but no blood splatter. They had searched but not found any other blood-covered clothing, either there or at his friend's house.

"Have you decided which pub you want to go to later?" Simon asked.

"You know them both. You can decide."

Peter turned to Rob's initial statement. Rob had promised to take Jane out that night, but an old friend turned up at work, and one drink had led to another. He described himself as slightly tipsy and merry when he arrived home later than planned, and Jane had accused him of being blind drunk. They argued, and Jane scratched his face and told him to get out. She had slammed the door after him, very much alive and furious.

The rest of the statement closely followed what Lucy had said. Rob walked to a local pub, the Tern Inn, where he stayed drinking for the rest of the night. At closing time, he sat on a bench to think about his options and fell asleep. After waking up feeling cold and stiff, he walked to his friend's house. He was woken the following morning by Duncan throwing a glass of water on him, saying he was leaving for work. He dragged himself off the sofa, took a cold shower to shock himself into life and walked home. He was still feeling drunk when he let himself into his house, but immediately sobered up when he found Jane.

"How late do you think we'll be finishing up, so I can let Kate know?" Simon asked.

"We'll have a better idea once we've spoken to Rob." Peter rubbed his eyes and nodded to his laptop. "What do you think so far?"

"The police have no concrete evidence against Rob, and his explanation is feasible," Simon said confidently. "Did you see that Jane's brother *did* accuse Rob of the murder? It looks like the police have decided Rob is guilty without any concrete evidence. I can't see any direct reference to the death of his first wife, but I think the local police have a history with Rob."

Peter was surprised Simon had been reading the file in between worrying about getting to the pub, as all he had seen him doing was staring into space. "I haven't read that far," he admitted. "How does Chris describe his sister's relationship?"

"Volatile, and he thought Jane was getting tired of Rob's drinking and irresponsibility," Simon said. "He thinks the main attraction for Rob was Jane's money."

"What did she do for a living?"

"She was a legal secretary."

Peter frowned. "I wouldn't have thought she earned that much. Possibly less than Rob earned as a car salesman if he was any good. Any clues as to what money he was referring to?"

Simon shook his head. "Who says he was a good salesman? A few lean months and who knows what their financial situation was."

"It's something we can easily find out," Peter said.

"If there isn't a magical pot of gold that we know nothing about, it suggests the brother had a low opinion of his sister," Simon said. "That, or he measures everything in financial terms. I don't like the sound of him."

Peter leaned back in his chair to stretch his back. "Who do you think we should see first?"

Simon eagerly snatched up a sheet of paper and walked over to sit next to Peter. "After Rob, Chris Forbes. He does seem to protest too much. I reckon there's a history there. Maybe they fell out about something else recently, and he saw an opportunity for revenge."

"Or he has good grounds for suspecting Rob of killing his sister," Peter said. "Who else?"

"The people in the pub and the friend who put him up for the night. It might be worth speaking to the Street Angels. I don't know if they operate that far out, but it's worth asking the question."

"Who are the Street Angels?"

"Volunteers who go out at night looking for people who are the worst for wear. Check they're okay and have a bed to go to. I've done a few shifts with them." When Peter raised a surprised eyebrow, Simon added, "Kate is big on us doing our bit for society."

"Good for you," Peter said, meaning it. He had recently thought of doing something useful with his spare time but never got around to it. Since leaving the force, he had become a bit of an insomniac, so the group would be worth looking into. "Any general thoughts about the assailant?"

"It was someone Jane knew, and he was looking for something. That ticks all the boxes for her brother. Maybe Chris had gone there asking for money, and things turned ugly when she refused."

"So the murder wasn't premeditated?"

"I would say not. The crime scene was erratic. The suspected weapon is a standard kitchen knife. Unlike his daughter, Rob couldn't say if one was missing from the kitchen drawers, but I don't think I could either. Kate has all sorts of different knives and corresponding chopping boards. She goes mental if I use the wrong one. I think she should label them if it's that important to her. Do you have different chopping boards?"

"I do, but back to the case," Peter said.

"The question is," Simon said. "Do we limit ourselves to proving Rob innocent, or do we want to find the real killer? If we do, as well as her brother, we need to investigate Jane and her other associates. A trusted legal secretary would be privy to many secrets. We should find out what type of law firm she worked for. Criminal Law or Commercial Law?"

"There are as many crooks in business as there are in the criminal courts," Peter said, looking at Simon with a begrudging respect. His mind jumped around all over the place, but he was smart. He had misjudged his lack of concentration because he had accepted Charlie's description of laziness. Simon was intelligent and quick-thinking, which made him impatient and quickly bored. Charlie was an old-school copper, methodical and pedantic, so it was easy to see how they clashed and misunderstood one another.

"Our remit is to establish Rob's innocence," Peter said. "To prove it might involve finding who was responsible, and Jane's place of work would be a good place to start, but let's take it one step at a time. After meeting Rob, I agree we should start with the people who can confirm his whereabouts the night Jane was killed. Then, speak to people Jane knew, including Chris. Depending on what we discover, we then consider whether to dig into her background."

"That'll work," Simon said.

CHAPTER SIX

Peter looked up from the file and checked the time. There was far more to Simon going on under the surface than Charlie indicated. He was sure Simon knew about his recent suicide attempt, but it hadn't hung between them as an unanswered question waiting to be addressed, as it did with so many people. It could be Simon was incredibly shallow and self-centred, but Peter didn't think that was the explanation. He was confused by the people-pleasing persona currently on display because he didn't think it was genuine. "I'll read the file for half an hour, and then we'll grab lunch."

"Great, time for another coffee," Simon said. "Are you happy with the lattes I've been making you? Charlie, the absolute philistine, wanted to make do with a kettle and instant, but I insisted on a decent machine. I can make anything you want."

Peter said, "Latte will be fine," and returned his attention to the file.

Simon collected the empty mugs scattered around the office and pushed open the door to the kitchen. Escaping from the shared space where he felt under surveillance to the small confines of the kitchen seemed a good idea when he first thought of it. It was somewhere he could feel safe and alone. Only when he walked in, the walls closed in around him like a coffin, suffocating and trapping him.

He put the dirty mugs on the counter and looked around. What the room needed was a window so he could look out at things. He swilled the mugs under the tap and set up the coffee machine before returning to the office. In the far corner of the room, he pulled open the top drawer of the heavy metal storage cabinet.

After noisily rummaging about, he found the file he was looking for and took it with him back to the kitchen.

Peter looked up when Simon placed a coffee mug next to him. "Thanks. Did you find what you were looking for?" When Simon looked blank, he nodded toward the metal cabinets. "You were looking for something in there."

Simon swivelled a chair around to sit next to Peter. "The building plans. We need a window in the kitchen. Do you want to come and have a look at where I think it should go?"

"No, I'm sure you know the building best."

"I was thinking it would be helpful when we have difficult cases to be able to look out at something."

All concentration lost, Peter leaned back and sipped his coffee. "What's behind the building?"

"Do you know, I'm not sure. An alleyway, I think."

"So, you would be looking at the wall of another building," Peter said, frowning.

"You're right. We also need a door so we can step outside. I'll go and get my coffee. Do you want to look at the plans?"

"Not really, no," Peter said. "When you return, can we concentrate on the case and how best to approach Rob?"

"Sure." When Simon returned, he sat at the far desk where he had been before.

Peter looked across and asked, "Any thoughts on why the police were so quick to think it was Rob? Was it only the circumstantial evidence?"

"I'll put my thinking cap on." Simon put his feet on the desk, leaned back in his chair and closed his eyes. Five minutes later, Peter's concentration was disturbed by Simon's snores. He shook his head and started to look at Rob's phone records.

CHAPTER SEVEN

Waiting for Rob in a cold, uninviting interview room, Peter said, "I'll lead the interview. If you think I've missed something, make a note of it and ask him at the end. Also, keep a lookout for any unusual reactions."

"I have done this before," Simon said. "Is it okay if I record it?"

"If he agrees, definitely."

Simon slowly looked around the sterile room. "I have a friend in interior design. They should give him a call."

"Soft furnishings and ambient lighting aren't high on their list of priorities. It's a bonus if they achieve minimum staff levels," Peter replied gruffly, hoping Simon wasn't going to pepper the interview with irrelevant comments. He was about to say something about it when the metal door clanged open, and Rob was led in.

It was obvious where Lucy's good looks came from. Rob had the same dark blond hair and face that you wanted to know more about. He looked physically fit, strong, and younger than the forty-nine years it said on his file. The main difference was that where Lucy had an air of vulnerability, he had an edge of danger, excitement, and fun. He smiled apologetically when he was led in wearing handcuffs to the chair, and two dimples appeared on his cheeks, making his face appear even younger.

"Thank you for seeing us. I'm Peter Hatherall, and this is Simon Morris. Your daughter has asked us to review the case to see if you should be in here."

"It's a relief to meet someone who doesn't automatically think I'm guilty. Even the brief they've appointed for me has taken their side. He keeps asking me the same boring questions over and over again. He is so wet behind the ears he's probably never had a long-term relationship, or drunk a skinful and lost a few hours along the way." Rob's voice was soft and rhythmical, and a smile danced across his face when he spoke. If his situation stressed him, it didn't show.

"I was going to ask you about your legal representation," Peter said. "If you don't feel he's helping, you should consider instructing someone yourself. Or, if money is a problem, at least request an alternative is appointed."

"I'll bear that in mind, but it seems unfair when I haven't done anything wrong. I'm as much the victim as Jane was." Rob beamed another huge smile, showing off his dimples. "Are you going to be able to help me?"

"We'll see," Peter said, distracted by the smiles and lack of anxiety. "To start, can you run through the events of the night of Jane's murder up until when you found her the next day?"

"Do you mind if I record this?" Simon asked.

Rob was happy to be recorded and started recounting his evening, which again closely followed his daughter's account. Peter interrupted him to ask for the names of every customer he recognised in both pubs, even if he only knew their first name. When Rob reached the point where he sat on the park bench contemplating life, Peter asked if he remembered calling his daughter.

Rob's face creased into an embarrassed smile. "Did I? I don't remember doing that."

"It's on your phone records."

"Then I must have done. I was in a bad way, and it's all a little fuzzy." Rob pulled some interesting faces as he stopped to think. "I don't remember making the call, but I've remembered something else. There was an old guy walking a small dog. A Jack Russell, I think. He shot me a disgusted look and scuttled past. I confess I shouted 'Boo,' to make him jump. Childish, I know. My only excuse is the drink. I'm sure it was that night. Hey, do you think he might remember me? I think I've seen him around before."

"Do you know where you've seen him before?"

Rob shrugged and smiled. "Just around, but he must be local. Crowcombe isn't a large place. You could find him."

"We'll try," Peter said. "And when you woke up on the bench and walked to your friend's house, did you pass anyone?"

Rob shook his head. "It might have been a Friday night, but I can confirm Crowcombe can't be described as a town that never sleeps." Rob laughed at his humour before continuing, "The area was dark and deserted. I probably wasn't that quiet. One of his neighbours might have heard me stumbling about. I vaguely remember knocking over some bins outside Duncan's house. He didn't mention hearing anything when he let me in, but it might have woken up one of his neighbours. Thinking about it, it was probably their bin. Other than that, it's one big blur."

CHAPTER EIGHT

Peter scribbled down some notes, more to give Rob a break than anything, until he moved on to the next set of questions. He closed the pad, and said, "I'm going to ask you about the morning now. When you found Jane."

Rob shuddered and looked serious for the first time. "Not a scene I want to revisit, but I'll do my best."

"When you arrived, but before you went in, did you notice anything unusual or out of place?"

After a pause and more face-pulling, Rob said, "The curtains were pulled. I thought that was strange. Jane rarely lies in, even on a weekend, and she always pulls them open as soon as she comes downstairs in the morning."

"Was the front door shut, and did your key work as usual in the lock?"

"Yes. Other than the curtains being drawn, everything was normal. Until I went in and found Jane, that is. It sounds a cliché, but it really did hit me like a stomach punch. All the air was knocked out of me. That vision comes back every night when I close my eyes. It will haunt me for the rest of my life." Rob's voice hardened, and he sounded bitter for the first time. "If I find out who did that to my beautiful Jane, I don't know what I'll do. He's an animal and a danger to everyone else. It's frustrating that they're wasting time on me when he's walking around. Free to do it again. It's not right." He turned and shouted to the officer who stood guarding the door. "Did you hear that? It's not right."

"Okay," Peter said calmly. "I know it's difficult, but can you focus on the scene? Did anything strike you as odd in the living room?"

"Other than my girlfriend lying dead on the floor in a pool of blood? Not really."

Ignoring the sarcasm, Peter asked, "And afterwards? Did the police ask you to check if anything was missing?"

"They did." Rob took a deep breath. His voice was neutral when he continued, and his smile had returned. "As far as I could tell, nothing was taken."

"What did you do next after you walked into the room?" Peter asked.

"Even though it was obvious, I checked to see if, by some miracle, Jane was alive. It was horrid. I've never touched a dead body before. I realised I was going to be sick just in time and ran to the downstairs toilet. I washed my face before returning to the living room and calling the police. I sat down next to Jane and waited for them to arrive. You'll think it dumb, but I didn't want her to wait all alone. Is that a bit odd?"

"Not at all. You'd had a terrible shock," Peter said. "What happened when they arrived?"

"To start with, they were considerate and kind to me. A constable sat with me in the kitchen. They reassured me that they would do everything possible to find the person responsible. Later, when Chris stuck his oar in, everything changed. And here I am while Jane's killer walks free."

"By Chris, I assume you mean Chris Forbes, Jane's brother?"

"Yes, that vindictive little creep," Rob said, his bitterness returning.

"I take it you don't get along?"

"I've barely spoken to him in all the years I've known Jane," Rob said. "He only appeared when he wanted more money and was always surly with me. He was never interested in seeing Jane. All he wanted was his money."

"Interesting, as he told the police that you were only interested in Jane's money," Peter said.

Rob laughed hollowly. "That sounds about right for him to automatically assume that everyone thinks the same way as him."

"Could you explain what money we're talking about?"

"Is this really necessary?" Rob sighed. "I don't know the full ins and outs of it. For that, you'll have to speak to someone else. The solicitor who set it all up, I suppose."

"Set what up?"

"The trust fund," Rob said, as if they should already know about it.

"Sorry, but this is the first we've heard about a trust fund. Do the police know about it?"

"I've assumed Chris has told them all about it - well, his version anyway," Rob said. But now you've mentioned it, I don't think they have asked me anything about it. I guess they don't think it's relevant."

"Could you tell us about it now?" Peter asked.

"All I know is when Jane's parents died, they didn't want to hand a lump sum to Chris because of his track record with money. He's a gambler and a drinker and had already blown thousands and lost his home. I think he rents a hovel somewhere now. Don't ask me where or what it's like. His inheritance was left in some sort of trust fund, and Jane was a trustee. I've no idea how much it is or what will happen to it now. It didn't involve me, so I never took much notice. All I know is he would turn up occasionally and demand she handed over some of his money."

"Do you know which firm of solicitors are handling the fund or who the other trustees are?"

"I haven't a clue. Maybe where she worked?" Rob suggested. "As far as I was concerned, it had nothing to do with me."

"Was Chris ever aggressive when he showed up asking for money?"

"Rude and arrogant is his default setting," Rob said. "Now that you've brought this up, I think you should check where Chris was that Friday night and whether he has any recent big losses. I bet the police haven't. I expect they were taken in by his posh voice."

"We have every intention of speaking with him," Peter said. "How about your financial situation? Car sales doing well?"

"So-so," Rob said. "New cars have taken a hit with Covid and then the cost of living, but the second-hand trade is buoyant. That's where I make most of my money, so yeah, I'm doing okay."

"Will your employers confirm that?" Peter asked.

"No reason why they shouldn't."

"Can you think of anyone else who might have called on Jane that night?" Peter asked. "Someone with a grudge or past issue?"

Rob shook his head. "I can't think of anyone. Until you got me thinking about Chris, I assumed it was some random stranger."

"Whoever it was, they either had a key or Jane let them in."

"That doesn't mean much, and I've gone over this with the police," Rob said. "My Jane had a big heart. She always fell for hard luck stories and would help anyone. If someone came to the door asking for help, to use the phone or the toilet maybe, she would let them in."

"Did she have friends or neighbours who regularly popped in?"

"Not really, no."

"How did your daughter Lucy get along with Jane?"

"Fine. I didn't date when Lucy was younger, and there was never any question of Jane trying to become her mother. I would say they rubbed along okay. More like friends or maybe work colleagues, you know. Polite and respectful but not besties," Rob said.

"Lucy spends her weekends at her boyfriend's," Peter said. "I wondered if there was an element of her feeling pushed out by your relationship with Jane. It's her house, isn't it?"

"No way. I wouldn't let something like that happen," Rob said, clearly affronted by the suggestion. "We discussed and agreed on the move together. The boyfriend is a recent thing. She's only been staying there very recently. We all got along fine."

"Okay," Peter said. "I'm going to ask you about the argument you had earlier that evening. As tests confirmed the skin under Jane's nails was yours, and you were sporting scratches on your face, I assume it was heated?"

"She was annoyed that I turned up late and thought I was too drunk to go out for the planned meal. I told her she was overreacting, and the restaurant wouldn't mind us being a little late, and it spiralled from there."

"It still seems rather dramatic. The neighbours said they heard shouting and crashing sounds."

"That would have been Jane throwing a mug at me. Followed by a saucepan."

"Did you often have heated arguments that ended up in fights?"

"I wouldn't call it a fight. A fight suggests I retaliated when I didn't. I merely ducked and dived." Rob looked sideways across the room and back at Peter. "Yes, it happened before, but not with any frequency. Maybe once or twice."

"Recently?"

"I guess," Rob said, sounding less sure of himself.

"What generally was the cause?"

Rob looked down. "Jane could be possessive. She didn't like me going out drinking with friends."

"Was it the friends or the drinking that was the problem?"

"A bit of both, but mostly the drinking," Rob admitted, looking up sheepishly.

"Would it be fair to say your relationship was going through a rough patch?"

"Possibly," Rob admitted before looking back at the floor.

"Were you close to splitting up?"

"No. We were going through an adjustment," Rob said carefully. "Moving from the honeymoon period to the more mundane. We were both in unchartered territory, but we would have worked it out."

"And if you didn't? If you were forced to move out, where would you go?"

Rob shrugged. "Rent somewhere, like I did before. It wouldn't be a big issue. Life goes on and all that. I'm not a violent person and would have accepted the situation and got on with my life. But it's irrelevant. We weren't about to break up. We were stronger than that."

"We'll leave that there for now, but we might have to talk about the state of your relationship again another time," Peter said.

"We understand from your daughter that her mother was killed in a car accident."

Rob's expression hardened, and he shook his head. "I don't see the relevance. Why drag that up?"

"A jury will, so we need to know," Peter said.

"Jury? It's not going to come to that. They haven't a shred of solid evidence against me. They'll have to let me go sooner or later. I'm hoping that you're going to make it sooner."

"We need to know what happened with your first wife," Peter calmly persisted.

"She was mown down by some joyriders when she was out shopping," Rob said. "The police found the burnt-out car a few days later but not the driver."

"Where were you at the time?"

"At a car auction in Birmingham. Is that good enough for you?" Rob asked. "I want to talk about Jane's murder. What happens next?"

Peter accepted it was best to leave the questions about Rob's first wife until he had more details. "We'll talk to a few people, try to trace the old man with the dog and see what we can find out."

"Including where Chris was that night?"

"Most definitely," Peter said. "Do you have any additional questions before we leave, Simon?"

Simon nodded. "You said you've never spent any time with Jane's brother. Why do you think he has accused you of killing his sister?"

Rob held his hands up, palms out. "Your guess is as good as mine. Although Jane was sympathetic towards him and made excuses for his rudeness, they didn't have a close relationship. I'm at a loss as to why he feels the way he does. Unless it's to divert suspicion away from himself."

"Would Jane have discussed your relationship problems with him?"

"We didn't have problems, but if we did, he's the last person she would speak to about them. The only person Chris cares about, is

Chris."

"Who would she confide in?" Simon asked.

"Her work friends, I guess," Rob said. "Caron and Clemmie were the two names that cropped up the most."

"Do you know the rest of her family?" Simon asked.

Rob shook his head. "Jane's parents died before we met."

"Uncles or aunts?"

"Oh, yes. There are a couple. They may be the other trustees you were talking about earlier. I've never met them, so I can't say any more than that."

"Why are the police convinced you killed Jane?" Simon asked directly.

After a moment of silence, Rob said, "They've put together our argument and my weak alibi and decided it had to be me. But it wasn't. I swear I would never hurt anybody like that, let alone my girlfriend."

"Have you ever been in trouble with the local police before this? Any reasons why they might automatically believe you could be responsible?"

"Years ago, when I was in my late teens, but nothing recent."

Simon looked down at his notes. "You said your solicitor also seems to think you're guilty, but you didn't give their name?"

"Edward Davies."

"I know him. I'll have a word," Simon said. "Did he say who he was working for?"

"I assumed me," Rob said, looking confused. "What happens now?"

"We've plenty of things to follow up on, and then we'll come back to you," Simon said.

Peter stood and collected his notes. "We'll be in contact once we've completed our initial enquiries."

CHAPTER NINE

Peter and Simon silently walked through security and onto Peter's car. Peter couldn't work Simon out. His questions proved he was intelligent and quick-thinking, yet at times he looked dazed, as if his mind was elsewhere. He waited until Simon shut his car door to ask, "What do you think now?"

"We need to know more about the state of their relationship, but I think he has a point about Chris diverting attention away from himself. There was obviously friction over the trust fund and how Jane held the purse strings. I think Chris is a good place to start. If the trust fund is wound up and he receives the balance, then there's his motive. I don't believe for one minute he would have volunteered that information to the police."

"I agree we need to see Chris, but before we get ahead of ourselves, I want to know how much money we're talking about and whether Jane's death makes any difference to the trust arrangement," Peter said. "Don't lose sight of the fact we have been asked to prove Rob's innocence. To do that, we should start with the people who can support Rob's alibi and then find someone who can comment on the dynamics between Rob, Jane and Lucy."

"You don't think Rob lost it that evening and killed her, do you?"

"I can understand why the police and Chris think it was him," Peter said, dodging the question. While he didn't rate the DCI in charge of the case, as an ex-copper, he didn't want to assume the police had got it so wrong by lazily relying on circumstantial evidence. He felt sure there would be a reason why the police were so confident that Rob was responsible.

"Putting it out there for the record," Simon said. "I don't think Rob is the type of person to be influenced by money."

"Everybody is to some extent," Peter said.

They returned to silence as Peter drove. It wasn't an uncomfortable silence, and Peter sensed Simon was thinking over the interview rather than stubbornly disagreeing with him. That, or he was daydreaming again.

Peter was unsure about the case. Meeting Rob had increased his doubts about his innocence, although it had also raised some interesting questions about Chris.

He was surprised that he hadn't seen any mention of a trust fund in the police report. It was possible that they didn't know anything about it, or had concluded it wasn't important. The ferocity of the attack and nothing being taken had led to the assumption the attack wasn't planned, but that could be wrong. The search through drawers could tie in with Chris looking for the trust documents. If Jane was the sole trustee and Chris now received the lump sum, he would be a prime suspect.

He desperately wanted to know more about Rob's first wife's death. It was a shocking coincidence, and he was surprised there was no mention of it in the police investigation. There was something off about the case, and he felt they were missing something. So much so that he would check they had received the whole file when they returned to the office.

He glanced across at Simon, silently staring out the window. It was disappointing that Rob didn't think his solicitor was very experienced as he had envisaged them working together on the case. "How do you know Rob's solicitor?"

"We've worked together before," Simon said.

"Rob didn't think much of him."

"His description was fairly accurate, but Ed is only a junior. He would have been sent out to gather information and report back to someone more senior, supervising the case."

"As you have previous contact, I'll leave you to liaise with them. Ask them what they're doing to help Rob's case. We'll be far more effective if we work together and don't duplicate things."

"Will do," Simon said, pulling out his phone. "I may as well ring him now." Ending the call, he asked, "Did you get the gist of that? Ed's done nothing other than speak to Rob, deal with a few procedural technicalities and prepare a report for the senior solicitor handling the case. Unfortunately, she's on a couple of days holiday. Meanwhile, Ed is sitting around twiddling his thumbs."

"Okay, so we're starting from scratch."

"Do you think it's possible Rob was so drunk that he killed Jane without remembering it?" Simon asked. "He didn't come across as a violent person or a guilty one."

"It's possibly a defence of last resort if the police gather enough evidence against him," Peter said. "But it's time we started to investigate rather than theorise. See if you can get hold of Duncan, the guy he stayed with Friday night. Failing that, try Jeremy, the friend he met after work. Their contact details are in the file."

"And if I can't get hold of either of them?"

"Check what time the pub opens."

"I told you," Simon said. "The Royal Oak is open all day if we're clocking off early."

"I meant the Tern Inn in Crowcombe - the pub Rob said he was in that Friday night," Peter said, exasperation slipping into his tone. There were so many things to consider and people to speak to, and all Simon could think about was relaxing with a drink.

"If it's the one I think it is, it won't be open until seven, possibly half past."

Peter chewed his lip, starting to wonder if Simon was an alcoholic. "You're very well acquainted with far-distant boozers."

Simon shrugged. "I've come across a few in my time. Okay, I had a girlfriend who lived out that way a few years back." Still holding his phone, he asked, "So, if I can't get hold of either of his friends, are we calling it a day?"

"No. We'll head back to the office. The report on Rob's first wife might have arrived," Peter said. "And you can formally register our involvement with the police if Charlie hasn't already done so, and introduce yourself."

Simon ended his calls, and said, "Well, that's super-efficient of me. Duncan will see us at his home as soon as we can get there, and Jeremy will meet us at a café just up the road from Duncan's in two hours. It's a gold star for me, I think. It will give you enough time to check for the report before we head to the pub. Maybe there I can persuade you to concentrate on Chris."

CHAPTER TEN

When they pulled up outside Duncan's mid-terrace house, there were very few cars in the street, so Peter could park right outside. Before opening his car door, Simon said, "Can I do the interview?"

"Be my guest," Peter said. He doubted Duncan had much to add other than confirming the state Rob was in that night, and it would be interesting to see Simon in action. He could always step in if Simon started to disappear along some strange tangent.

Duncan opened the front door in black trousers and a white button-down shirt. He was handsome, clean-shaven and about the same age as Rob. "Come in. I'll make you a coffee and then go upstairs to change if that's okay. I've just returned from work."

"Sure," Peter said. "What work do you do?"

Duncan led them into a kitchen. "I'm a train guard, so my hours are a little all over the place. Good job you caught me today, as I'm on proper earlies starting from tomorrow." Duncan chatted away about the state of the railways while he made three coffees before disappearing upstairs. The kitchen was a disorganised mess of takeout boxes and unwashed cutlery. It was functional with no personal touches, and Peter assumed correctly that Duncan lived alone.

Duncan reappeared in tatty jeans and a T-shirt advertising a heavy metal band. Leaning against the kitchen units, he took a slurp of his coffee left on the side. "What can I tell you about that night except Rob arrived late and crashed on the sofa? I barely knew his girlfriend, and I haven't seen much of Rob either in the last few years, to be fair."

"How long have you known each other?" Simon asked.

"Since forever," Duncan said. "We were at school together all the way through from infants. After we left school, we spent much more time together. Well, drinking together, if I'm honest. A right couple of hellraisers we were back then. Or thought we were, anyway.

"That all stopped when his wife was knocked down, and he was left with the kid. He took that responsibility seriously and cleaned his act up. Dedicated to her, he was. We only got back in contact a few years ago. It was when his daughter was at college, I think. He was right proud of her, but he was also sad they were growing apart. He was looking for company and wanted to pick up where we left off. The only thing is, with my job, I have to be careful and pick and choose my times for a good night out. They constantly check us for alcohol and drugs. Instant dismissal if we're caught out with anything in our system."

"You're drinking partners as much as anything?"

Duncan shrugged his agreement. "We've had some cracking nights, though."

"You must have known his first wife."

"Yeah, Emily. Cracking girl." Duncan picked up his coffee mug and joined them around the table. "She liked a drink and could drink most men under the table." Duncan shook his head sadly. "Such a shame. It shook us all up. I remember her funeral like it was yesterday. I don't think her family were too impressed when we all threw bottles of whisky in on top of the coffin. She would have appreciated that, even if her snobby family were horrified and refused to have us at their fancy wake. We took some bottles down to the river and remembered her in our own way."

"Were they a wealthy family?" Simon asked.

"I wouldn't say super wealthy, but they had a bob or two spare. A couple of swanky five-star holidays abroad a year, weekends at country clubs and smart cars. You know, the type who believes everything they read in the Daily Mail. Emily hated it. She much preferred roughing it with us lot. Just before the accident, her Gran had died and left her a hefty sum. She had some crazy idea of buying a farm and us all living together as some sort of commune. She didn't want to keep it herself. Said money corrupts people. I guess she meant her parents."

"What happened to the money after she died?" Simon asked. "Did you ever buy that farm?"

"No," Duncan said with a laugh. "I dunno where it went. Maybe it went back to the family, or Rob had it. Like I said, I stopped seeing so much of him around that time."

"They never caught the driver who knocked her down," Simon said.

Duncan leaned forward and said conspiratorially, "There was talk of it being gang related. Emily was a wild one and didn't limit herself to whisky. It was said in certain circles she had started a little dealing on the side. No idea if that's true, but you could tell towards the end she was using quite heavily."

"And where was Rob when this was going on?"

"Drunk as a skunk, mostly. You have to remember we were little more than kids at the time," Duncan said. "But after Emily died, Rob pulled himself together. He had to for the kid. I saw him to wave to from time to time when he was walking the kid home from school, but that was about it."

"And then he got back in contact with you?" Simon asked.

"Yeah, a couple of years ago, but it's not as easy as before because I have to fit things in around my shifts, and neither of us is getting any younger. I can't shrug off the hangovers like I used to."

"Has he turned up at your door needing somewhere to sleep before?"

"In the old days, yes."

"But not recently?" When Duncan shook his head, Simon asked, "Why do you think it was your door he knocked on that night?"

Duncan shrugged. "I was closest."

"How was he when you opened the door? Did he say anything?"

"He was seven sheets to the wind. He slurred something about Jane kicking him out, staggered to the sofa and collapsed onto it," Duncan said. "I had been fast asleep, so I left him there to sleep it off and went back to bed."

"Do you remember what he was wearing?" Simon asked.

"Yes, but the police already asked me this. Jeans and a denim shirt. And he wasn't covered in blood. That, I would have noticed and assumed he had been in a fight."

"With Jane?"

"No, I would have assumed he had gotten into a pub brawl."

"Was that something that happened when he was out drinking?" Simon asked.

"Not recently, but he would always have your back in a fight in the old days. We would get into scrapes on some of our nights out when we were kids, but that was because we were often drunk and annoying. I don't remember him ever setting out to start a fight on purpose, and he's never been the short-tempered or stressed type."

"When you've been out with him, how does he treat women generally?"

"Oh, he's always been a regular Mr Charmer," Duncan said, smiling. "He has all the chat-up lines, but he's respectful with it. The women always lap it up. You would know what I mean if you've ever seen him with his daughter. He treats her like a princess."

"And what was he really like with women? Once he got to know them better?"

"About the same, to be honest. I don't know much about Jane, but he put Emily on a pedestal. You knew not to disrespect his girl in earshot. Then he was the same with his kid."

"How was Emily towards him?"

"They were very much in love. He was devastated by her death. Lucky, I guess, that he channelled all his hurt into caring for his daughter. Who knows where he would have ended up otherwise? The same place, probably."

"Was Rob ever blamed for her death?"

"Only by her family, which was rubbish. They blamed Rob for leading her astray, but she had rejected their lifestyle long before meeting Rob."

"And away from women, was Rob ever aggressive?"

"No, he's always been laid-back and happy-go-lucky."

Simon straightened in his chair and looked directly at Duncan. "Do you think Rob attacked Jane while drunk?"

Without batting an eyelid, Duncan replied, "No way. Not in a million years."

CHAPTER ELEVEN

After spending longer than they anticipated with Duncan, when Simon and Peter arrived at the café, Jeremy was outside looking at his watch. He was an eccentric character, colourfully dressed in purple canvas trousers while his football-shaped stomach strained against the buttons of his yellow shirt. He greeted them enthusiastically and waved away their apologies for being late as they went inside.

Once they had ordered coffees and settled into their seats, Jeremy asked, "What more do you want to know about that night? I've told the police everything I could think of. It should all be in my statement somewhere, but if there's anything else I can help you with, then let me know."

Simon looked at Peter, who indicated he should go ahead with the interview. "How do you know Rob?"

"I knew Rob back in the old days when we first found our way into dealing cars. We used to bump into each other at the auctions - or maybe I should say the bars afterwards." Jeremy laughed to himself. "Back then, I wouldn't be surprised if he stole a few cars to order. Of course, it's all different now."

"The trade or Rob?" Simon asked.

"Both. He works for a big company now. As far as I know, everything is above board."

"And yourself?"

"I still work for myself, finding people cars, although it's getting harder these days. I'll hang up my keys soon. Rather that, than sell my soul to one of the big dealerships like Rob."

"But you stayed in contact?"

"Not really, no. We bumped into one another by chance the

other day. I probably hadn't seen him for ten years or so before that. But we hit it off straight away, just like in the old days and decided to have a few beers together."

"Had he changed much?"

"A bit older, but essentially the same. I can't say as I knew him that well before."

"Did you know his first wife, Emily?"

"I didn't even know he was married. Thinking back, he used to chat all the women up but never took it any further, so I should have guessed."

Simon looked to Peter, questioning whether there was any point continuing, and Peter asked, "Who suggested you go out for a drink?"

Jeremy frowned. "Rob, I think, but that was where the conversation was heading, anyway. We were catching up on the trade and old faces. We had a couple of pints, then a couple of shots before leaving to go our separate ways."

"Did Rob mention anything about his personal life?" Peter asked.

"He talked about his daughter and said he was living with someone," Jeremy said. "That's how the chat ended. He said he was running late for a meal."

"How would you describe Rob that evening?" Peter asked.

"The same as always. Entertaining and chatty. Maybe a little more chilled than I remember. He certainly didn't seem anxious to be anywhere else."

"Do you remember what he was wearing?"

"Later in the pub?" Jeremy queried. "Jeans and a denim shirt, I think."

"Why do you say, later in the pub?" Peter asked.

"He was wearing dark trousers and a white shirt when I bumped into him earlier. I guess he had the change of clothes at work."

"You met him earlier in the day and arranged to meet later? That wasn't clear from the police statement we've seen," Peter said.

"Yes. I bumped into him at lunchtime. He had a pre-booked appointment, so we arranged to meet up after he finished work," Jeremy said. "I thought I made that clear before."

"Thanks for clarifying that," Peter said, doubting it made much difference. "Do you remember anything about the death of his first wife?"

"Only what I heard on the grapevine at the time. I was surprised to hear he was married. I looked out for him afterwards to say how sorry I was, but he wasn't about."

"Do you remember what was being said at the time?"

"There was a rumour that it wasn't a simple hit-and-run. All sorts of nonsense, from how she was targeted by the local drug lord to how Rob had paid for her to be killed. But I didn't take too much notice of that. I think much of it was fuelled by Rob disappearing off the scene afterwards. You know how people gossip, adding extra bits from their imagination with every retelling."

"But you never believed any of it?"

"I wouldn't have hung around with him if I did," Jeremy said. "He had a reputation for being a little wild in his youth. And maybe he did steal the odd car. That's also only a rumour, by the way. But kill someone? No, that's not the Rob I knew. He had to make a living, we all do, but I've never heard of him ripping anyone off. He liked to pretend he sailed pretty close to the wind, but he mostly played by the rules and was always fair. As to his private life - I was never privy to it, but he didn't strike me as a violent person."

Peter leaned forward to shake Jeremy's hand. "Thank you very much for your time. If you think of anything later that might be useful, give us a ring."

"Will do." Jeremy stood and handed over his card. "When you're ready to upgrade your car, give me a ring first. I'll sort you out with something decent."

Walking from the café, Peter said, "As we're not far away, how about we check whether the Tern Inn is open?"

Simon checked the time and said, "We're still a little early."

"They may have changed their opening times since you were there last," Peter said. "Even if they're shut, the landlord might be around and remember something about the night Rob was in and who the man walking his dog late at night was."

CHAPTER TWELVE

The Tern Inn was a modern, purpose-built pub decorated to look older with moulded beams, black-and-white framed prints on the wall and dimmed lighting. And it was open. The girl behind the bar efficiently poured their pints but looked blank when Peter asked her about Rob and shot off to find Dave, who they assumed was the landlord or manager. When Dave appeared wearing his manager's name badge, Peter wasn't convinced he was old enough to even be in a pub. However, he couldn't deny they kept a good pint of ale.

Dave could remember the evening of the murder and said everyone in the area did. "Nothing of that magnitude has ever happened around here before. We're a quiet pub in a residential area, serving the local community. We only get busy for major football and rugby games unless someone has booked out the back room for a party. Nothing was on that night, so it was a standard Friday night. There were a few stragglers by closing time, but we were mostly empty."

"Did you see Rob that night and was it usual for him to be in?" Peter asked.

"I did," Dave confirmed. "It wasn't unusual for Rob to have a few beers on a weekend night, but it was unusual for him to drink alone until closing. He mostly comes in here with a group for the football matches. Occasionally, he'll come in by himself but only for a couple of pints earlier in the evening."

"Did you speak to him that night?" Peter asked.

"Only when serving him, and it was nothing more than the usual, 'How are you doing?' I can vaguely remember him grimacing and saying something about domestic problems."

"Can you be any more exact about what he said?"

"Not really. It was along the lines of can't live with women, can't live without them.' It was enough for me to realise he had recently argued with Jane but nothing specific."

"But he was in all evening, alone?" Simon asked.

"He came in somewhere between eight and nine o'clock, and at one point, I thought he would never leave. I couldn't swear to it, but I'm fairly sure he didn't leave and return during the evening." Dave pointed to a bar stool set back a short distance from the bar. "That's where he sat. Although I was busy with other things and changed a few barrels in the cellar, no one except him sat there."

"Do you know anyone in the area who walks a terrier-type dog late at night around here?" Peter asked.

"Sorry, I can't help you there. On an average evening, all I see are these four walls," Dave said. "We used to let people bring their dogs in, but there was one too many incidents with dogs fighting and knocking over drinks. Can't say as I remember someone coming in with a terrier."

"You've never seen anyone out walking when you lock up?"

"Can't say as I have."

"Is there anyone else in the pub now who was in that night?" Peter asked.

Dave stood and looked around the near-empty pub. "Can't see anyone. Your best bet would be to come back on a Friday night. The regulars here are creatures of habit. Or check with the police. I think they had a list of everyone who was in that night."

The girl from behind the bar appeared at the table. "Sorry to interrupt, but one of the beers needs changing."

"Go ahead," Peter said to Dave. "Thanks for your help. We'll come back if we need anything else."

"My pleasure," Dave said. "Would you like a round on the house? Tilly will sort you out."

"Thank you. Another pint of this for me, please," Peter said, turning his glass to show the brand name.

Simon said, "A pint of Guinness, please."

When Dave and Tilly left, Peter said, "You didn't like your Doombar, then? I told you to try the Bonville Pale. It's brewed locally."

"I thought there was a rule about policemen taking freebies?"

"I'm no longer with the police," Peter said.

After their drinks arrived, Simon asked, "What's the plan for tomorrow?"

"I know you're keen to interview Chris, but we should go together once we're armed with details about the trust fund. That's where I'm going to start, tomorrow. I also want to know if Rob gained financially from his first wife's death. Why don't you start by researching Chris, especially his gambling habit? Maybe see if you can speak to some of Jane's work colleagues. Meet at the office after lunch? Say two o'clock?"

"Works for me," Simon said. "What are you doing about eating this evening?"

"I'm not sure they do food here. If they do, I doubt it's up to much." Peter lifted his pint. "They do, however, serve an excellent beer. Somebody knows what they're doing in the cellar. Shame I don't live closer, and I have to drive home."

"Why don't you come back with me? Kate loves cooking for people."

"Without any notice, I very much doubt it. Save that for another evening. *After* you've asked her."

"I'll hold you to that," Simon said. "After hearing what his friends say about him, do you still think Rob could be guilty?"

"I'm keeping an open mind," Peter replied. "But unexpected things can happen in the heat of an argument. People lash out, especially if drink is involved."

"I'm also keeping an open mind, but I think he's innocent," Simon said.

Noticing Simon's empty glass, Peter finished his pint, and said, "Come on then. Time to get home."

When Peter pulled up outside the office to let Simon out, he said, "I just want to pop in and pick up my laptop and check to see if the report on Rob's first wife has arrived."

Simon said, "I may as well come in with you." As soon as he unlocked the door, Peter retrieved his laptop to check his e-mails.

"Funny how things turn out, isn't it?" Simon called from the kitchen. "Do you want another latte? I expected Jeremy to be a mine of information and Duncan to be unable to add much. But it turned out the other way around. I wonder what Kate is up to."

Peter tried to block out Simon's chat and concentrate. "Hey! I've got the report on the hit-and-run."

"Why didn't you check for it on your phone? I use mine for most things."

Scrolling through the report, Peter said, "I've additional security on here." Without looking up, he added, "Rob was questioned about the hit-and-run accident."

Simon emerged from the kitchen and placed a coffee mug next to Peter. "Where was he at the time?"

"According to this, at a car auction in Birmingham, collecting a car for a customer, like he said. They checked it out, and the timings worked, but that doesn't mean he didn't arrange the accident and make sure he had a watertight alibi."

Simon slid into the adjacent seat. "Or he's been terribly unlucky. Emily was living dangerously if she was dealing on someone else's patch. Was there any investigation into that rumour?"

Peter scrolled backwards and forwards, squinting at the screen. "Doesn't look like it."

"Charlie is stubborn about wearing his glasses," Simon said.

"What? I don't need glasses," Peter said, leaning back to drink his coffee. "It's interesting that they thought checking his alibi was worthwhile. They obviously had their suspicions."

"Same force?"

"Yes," Peter replied. "I'll ask for a copy of his records tomorrow. He admitted to having some run-ins in the past."

"No need. Charlie already did," Simon said. "It's in his notes for us. Mostly minor offences like drunken behaviour, but he did steal a few cars in his teens. Not for resale, though. Joyriding and racing with mates. A big leap from that to arranging for his wife to be mown down."

Peter said over the rim of his coffee mug, "We have a pattern though of wealthy partners meeting a violent end. It's too late to contact solicitors, but tomorrow I'll find out where Emily's inheritance went and look at the terms of Jane's will."

"And her brother Chris and the trust fund," Simon said.

Peter closed his laptop and packed it back into his backpack. He drank the last of his coffee, and said, "Well, I'm done for tonight. See you back here tomorrow."

CHAPTER THIRTEEN

When Simon pulled into Holly Bush Farm, Kate was returning from walking the dogs. As soon as he opened the car door, the three dogs greeted him joyously, jostling for attention.

"How did it go?" Kate asked.

"Good. Better than I expected, to be honest," Simon said, scratching Albert behind the ears. "I thought he would be as stuffy as Charlie, but he's nowhere near as bad."

Kate gave Simon a playful thump as they walked into the house. "Charlie isn't stuffy. He's mostly exasperated by you. Without him to keep you on the straight and narrow, you probably wouldn't have a business."

"I know. I know," Simon said. "But he does enjoy doing all those boring things."

"Like basic admin," Kate said. "I expect he would appreciate your help from time to time."

"Did his flight get away on time?"

"Yes, and he's called to say he's landed okay, but stop changing the subject."

"Good. Let's hope he has a fantastic time, and we have a solved case when he gets back," Simon said. "Mmm, something smells delicious."

"I wouldn't get too excited. It's a vegetable stew warming in the slow cooker. I've been busy getting organised for my trip," Kate said. "Are you going to be okay while I'm away?"

"Yes. Why wouldn't I be?"

"I don't know. You've been on edge recently." Kate hesitated. She had planned on leaving things until her return but decided to continue as she had started. "Is something bothering you?"

"No. When did you say that stew will be ready?"

"It will be ready whenever you're hungry."

"I'm always hungry. Shall we have it now? I invited Peter back for something to eat, but he said I had to give you some pre-warning."

"I'm warming to him already," Kate said. "Invite him over when I'm back. While I'm away, you can do some detecting. Like is he vegetarian or vegan, and does he have any dietary issues? Knowing what he likes and detests would be a bonus."

"Leave it with me," Simon said, oblivious to Kate's sarcastic tone. "Shall I open a bottle of wine?"

Eating their supper at the table, Kate asked, "What is the case you're working on? I asked Charlie, but he was already in holiday mode and told me to ask you."

"It's the case that was in the news a while back. Jane Forbes, the woman stabbed in her home. The police are charging her boyfriend, Rob with her murder. Our client is his daughter. She wants us to prove he is innocent."

"Is he?"

"I think so. The evidence against him is circumstantial, and Jane's brother looks a far more likely candidate. He has gambling debts, and their parents set up a trust for them, with Jane holding the purse strings. I'll be working from home tomorrow morning, delving into his background."

"Does Peter think the same way about the brother?"

"He has a few doubts about Rob's innocence, but I aim to eliminate them tomorrow," Simon said.

"I see storm clouds ahead for your new bromance." Kate raised an eyebrow. "While you're concentrating on proving your new partner wrong, what's he going to be doing?"

"He's looking at the financial implications of Jane's death. I think he'll find the trust money will be released to her brother, and voila, there's his motive." Simon quietly added, "We discovered Rob's first wife was killed years ago in a hit-and-run accident. Peter thinks it might be relevant."

"Was she wealthy?"

Simon shrugged. "Possibly."

Kate shook her head in despair. "Don't let it become a competition and lose track of the truth."

"We won't! We agreed to carry out our independent enquiries and meet up after lunch to discuss our findings. We're working as a team, tackling it from different directions," Simon said. "It's a pleasant evening. Do you want to walk the dogs down to the pub for a drink?"

Peter arrived home to telephone messages from his daughter Amelia and Fiona, his old DI, both wanting to know how his first day working with Simon had gone. He made himself a coffee and sat in his favourite armchair in his snug to ring Amelia. It was a short call as she was getting ready for a date. He was proud of Amelia and her success in her catering business, but he wanted to see her happily settled down with someone. She was coy about who she was meeting, and he didn't push it. If it turned out to be someone special, she would tell him in her own time. Whether he would resist running a check on them was another matter. He finished his coffee and called Fiona.

"Hi, how did it go?" Fiona asked. "Did you get along with Simon okay?"

"He's an odd one, but we got along better than I expected," Peter said. "I can see why he rubs Charlie up the wrong way. They're polar opposites. Simon is smart, but he lacks discipline and focus."

Fiona laughed. "I'm sure you're already plotting how you're going to whip him into shape. And the case you're investigating?"

"Interesting," Peter replied. "A guy has been charged with killing his girlfriend, and his daughter wants us to prove he didn't do it. I have a lot to follow up on. Do you know DI Andy Ford? He handled the initial investigation."

"No, I've not come across that name," Fiona replied. "Who was the DCI?"

"Jack Harris?"

"Oh. Did you know he was involved before you agreed to take the case on?"

"No, but I won't let it colour my judgement," Peter said.

"Are you sure about that?"

"I admit I would love to settle some old scores and prove him wrong, but I'm only interested in discovering the truth. I will be very civil if our paths cross, but I'm hoping to deal directly with the DI."

"Do you think they've made a mistake?"

"Simon certainly does, which is why I'm letting him run with looking at alternative explanations. I haven't made up my mind, but I've yet to establish why they have charged the boyfriend on what seems to be circumstantial evidence. I can only assume the police know more than is detailed in the reports."

"Sadly with murder, it often is the partner," Fiona said.

"And his attitude to women concerns me, even if his family and friends are taken in by it."

"How do you mean?"

"On the surface, he puts them on pedestals and treats them like princesses," Peter said. "There's money involved as well. Potentially a lot."

"It all sounds very intriguing," Fiona said. "I need to be somewhere in half an hour, so I've got to go. We'll catch up properly soon."

"Sure. Speak soon."

Peter ended the call and wandered into his newly fitted-out kitchen. It seemed too alien and pristine clean as he checked inside the neatly organised food cupboards. Finding nothing he vaguely fancied, he decided to walk down to the local pub for something to eat. Afterwards, he would spend the evening shifting through everything he could find about Rob's first marriage.

CHAPTER FOURTEEN

Simon rolled out of bed when he heard Kate returning from walking the dogs. Another hour in bed was tempting, but he wanted to say goodbye properly before she left. He stumbled and stubbed his toe on the bedframe in his rush to get dressed. Hopping around in pain made his head throb even more. With every hop, his stomach churned, and he regretted having that last pint a little more.

If he had been sensible, he would have called it a night when Kate did, but he hadn't seen Gladys and Dick in months, and they were always such fun. Neither of them was prepared to forgo drinking to drive, so they tended to stick with their local pub, which he didn't like.

As Simon pulled on his jeans, he wondered if they had managed to cycle home safely. He had offered their spare bedroom to them, but they had been determined to cycle.

Kate turned away from the stove when he stumbled bleary-eyed into the kitchen. "You look dreadful. How many more drinks did you have after I left?"

"Too many," Simon groaned.

"I'm making porridge. Do you want some?"

"No, thanks." Simon sat at the table with his head in his hands while Albert and Alfred sat on either side of him with their heads in his lap, sensing his pain. "Could you make me a coffee?"

Kate placed a coffee next to him. "Once I've eaten, I'll be off. Are you sure you don't want me to take all three dogs with me?"

Simon lifted his head and wrapped his hands around the coffee mug. "We'll be fine."

"You'll need to get up early to walk them before work."

"I know. I know." Simon sipped his coffee. "Once I've drunk this, I'll be raring to go."

Kate brought her bowl of porridge to the table and started eating. "I'll only be gone a couple of nights. Try not to get into any trouble while I'm gone."

"I'll be on my best behaviour. Scouts' honour," Simon said, saluting her.

"How did Gladys and Dick get home? I thought you were going to ask them back."

"I did, but they wanted to cycle. They had spent all day getting their bikes ready and didn't want it to go to waste."

"I'll call them before I leave to check they arrived home safely and aren't in a ditch somewhere. Good job you're not meeting Peter until after lunch. At least you'll have time to sober up before then."

Simon straightened up, rubbed his eyes and slurped his coffee. "I have a few hours to pull something together for him, and I made a start last night. Dick has a friend who is a bookie. He's going to call him later to see if he knows Jane's brother."

"Shouldn't you have run that by Peter first? You know what Dick is like. He's hardly discreet." Kate finished her porridge, and added, "Chances are Dick won't remember your conversation if he was as drunk as you were."

"Making good use of contacts is what it's all about," Simon said. "But I will call Dick later to remind him and ask he uses his discretion. So, no need for you to ring them as well. Will that make you happy?"

"It's not about making me happy," Kate said, getting up from the table and taking her empty bowl to the sink. She rinsed the bowl and called Popeye from her bed. "Well, I'll be off now. See you in a couple of days."

Simon jumped up to give Kate a goodbye hug and kiss. "Sorry if I got a bit carried away last night. I'll miss you."

"Good, but I still need to get a move on, or I'll be late. I'll see you in a couple of days."

Simon followed Kate to her car, picking up her bags and

Popeye's feed bowls on the way. He stood barefoot on the drive, enthusiastically waving her goodbye. When her car disappeared from the driveway and around the bend, he stepped back and slumped against the wall. Ruffling Albert's coat, he said, "I still feel rough. I think a half-hour nap before I start my research would be a good idea." He wandered back inside with his dogs on his heels, grabbed a couple of painkillers from the kitchen drawer and headed for his favourite couch in the snug, which he used as his office.

The dogs barking at the postman woke him a couple of hours later. He quickly jumped up, checked the time and switched on his laptop. Unsure where to start researching Chris Forbes, he called Dick. By the sounds of it, Dick was still in bed and had no recollection of the previous night's conversation about his bookie friend. Simon quickly reminded him of their agreement and asked that Dick give a vague explanation of receiving a tip from Chris in a pub for why he was interested in finding out more about his track record.

Not expecting to find anything of note, Simon completed a Google search for Chris Forbes. He was surprised to find a whole host of entries. A quick scroll suggested many of them related to large bets on individual horse races, but there were several newspaper articles. The recent ones related to Jane's death, but there was an older article about him losing his home. With only an hour before he had to leave to meet Peter, he decided to focus on the article about his eviction - but first, he needed more coffee.

Simon stretched out on the couch with his coffee on a side table and his laptop on his legs and started to read. The unflattering photograph of Chris Forbes, bloated and red-faced, standing outside a large Edwardian detached house set the tone for the news article and quickly had Simon searching for a pen and paper to make a note of the journalist's name.

The writer was clearly revelling in the dramatic fall from grace of the man he referred to as an over-privileged idiot and how his neighbours were pleased to see the back of him. There had been a crowd to watch Chris being forcibly removed from the property, and Simon wondered if the journalist had arranged it that way. The whole article smacked of a personal grudge and revenge.

The house and ten acres of surrounding land had been given to Chris by his parents for his twenty-first birthday, but he had mortgaged it to cover his spiralling gambling debts. Among the gleeful crowd watching the spectacle was the local pub landlord who claimed to be owed thousands. Egged on by the crowd, Chris had thrown a punch, which resulted in a successful assault charge being brought by one of the bailiffs. Simon added the names of the pub landlord and the bailiff to his list of people to contact.

Surprised that over an hour had passed, he looked up the firm of solicitors Jane had worked for. It was a small general practice in Crowcombe. He couldn't see the friends Rob had mentioned, but Jane was listed as a paralegal specialising in personal injury. He doubted the pay was much different from that of a legal secretary, but it indicated that Jane was ambitious and wanted to further her career.

In her company headshot, Jane looked full of vitality, younger and far more attractive than in Rob's photographs. Simon was saddened to think the smartly dressed woman confidently smiling on the company website had met such a violent end. Some men feared strong women. Could her career aspirations have been the cause of their recent arguments? And her death? He quickly dismissed the idea as he was positive Rob was innocent.

Accepting he had run out of time if he was going to meet Peter by two o'clock, he closed his laptop, promised his dogs he would be back soon and headed to his car. At least he had something to show for the morning. He could easily elaborate on the little research he had done. He didn't know why he wanted to impress Peter, only that he did. It could be because he was so different to Charlie and was prepared to listen to his ideas and give him a chance. Or maybe it was because he was a new person that he hadn't let down yet.

CHAPTER FIFTEEN

Peter woke up in the armchair in his dining room with a stiff back just as it was getting light. Another night where he had failed to make it upstairs to bed. It was becoming something of a habit. He had set to work as soon as he returned from the pub, and the table was littered with his handwritten notes and reminders.

He stood and circled his hips to unlock his stiff back muscles so he could stand straight. He checked through a few of his notes and looked up at the clock. He would have to wait until nine o'clock to ring the two firms of solicitors he had noted down.

The first was Hendricks Solicitors in Nettlebridge, who had handled Emily Walford's estate after the fatal hit-and-run. Walford Haulage and Warehousing Company was listed among its major clients. Additional research revealed that Emily's grandfather had founded it, and it currently employed over three hundred. The inheritance Duncan had mentioned was from Emily's grandmother, so it would have been personal and could have been anything from very modest to substantial.

He searched through his pile of scribbled notes for the printout of the newspaper article on Emily's accident. Nothing in the article or anywhere else referred to any speculation about the cause other than it was a random hit-and-run with no obvious suspects. A grainy photograph showed that Emily had been blonde, short and plump, while Jane had been brunette, tall and thin. He hated to make assumptions, but purely on looks, the two women had nothing in common other than coming from wealthy families.

The second firm, Foxfields Solicitors, were the Forbes family's solicitors. They specialised in administering large estates and inheritance tax planning. It was hard to tell from the crime scene photographs but Jane's living room had looked tastefully decorated without being exceptional. He wondered where all the money had gone if she had received a substantial inheritance from her parents. Maybe the tax avoidance scheme hadn't gone to plan?

Last night, he had been about to search for copies of the wills when he moved to the armchair to rest his eyes for half an hour and fell asleep. It was unclear whether Jane had a will, but he assumed any work on it would be held up until the police completed their investigations.

Peter rubbed his back. His back muscles were starting to ease, but he felt groggy from his night of broken sleep in the armchair. He decided to shower and eat some breakfast to clear his brain fog before continuing his research.

After his shower, he couldn't resist stopping to look out of the top landing window towards the next-door house where his previous girlfriend had lived before returning to France after the birth of her first grandchild. If it came to it, he might prioritise Amelia's needs over those of a new partner, but he wouldn't throw everything away for her unless he was already looking for an excuse to end the relationship. And that was why it hurt. He thought he and Nicole had something worthwhile. He'd obviously thought wrong. His thoughts turned to Sally and the twins, who now called Sally's new partner Dad. That hurt, too. He rested his hands on the windowsill as he looked down.

The 'For Sale' sign and his hopes Nicole would return, were long gone. The sign had been quickly replaced by the 'Sold' sign, followed by excited cries and a removal van and now the front garden was littered with tricycles and a trampoline. A young family with everything to look forward to, while he was the lonely, grumpy, middle-aged man living next door. How that transition had happened to him so quickly was beyond him. He pushed himself away from the window and determined his daily allowance for wallowing in self-pity was spent.

Downstairs, he made himself a strong coffee and some toast and carried his breakfast to the dining room table. He requested copies of the two earlier wills online, disappointed to discover there would be a delay of ten days. Last night, he had optimistically thought he would only have to wait a day at most. Bureaucracy had moved slowly within the police force, but it resembled a funeral march outside of it. Everything took forever, including the clock hands slowly clicking around to nine o'clock.

Accepting there was nothing he could do but wait, he wandered out to the garden to finish his coffee. There was a slight chill in the air, but the promise of spring was there in the birdsong and bluebells, and he was sure he had heard a cuckoo earlier. He watched a robin hopping from branch to branch at the far end of the garden before being chased off by a blackbird. He held himself still while a woodpecker landed a few feet from him and pecked at the ground until he was also chased off by the blackbird. Finishing his coffee, he spotted a fox slinking past his garden shed and smiled. He raised his coffee cup to it in celebration of it evading the hunt for another season, before he returned inside with an improved mood. He had made a lot of mistakes over the years, but moving out to the cottage wasn't one of them.

When the clock ticked one minute past nine, he rang Hendricks Solicitors to ask about Emily Walford's will. The woman who answered firmly said they wouldn't release any information over the phone, but if he presented himself at their offices with official identification, she would see what limited details she could provide.

Charlie had registered the company with the Association of British Investigators, insisted Peter complete an online data protection workshop and given him a supply of personalised cards. Hoping that would be enough to satisfy the solicitor, he made an appointment for ten o'clock.

He rang Foxfield Solicitors, hoping they would be equally willing to see him. They bluntly said they couldn't release Jane's will or meet him any time soon to discuss the contents, but they let slip some interesting details. Jane's parents had left everything to her, with no mention of her brother or a trust fund. Chris, Rob and Lucy had instructed solicitors to represent them in relation to Jane's will, which partly explained why they didn't want to be troubled by any more interested parties.

He didn't have time to call Lucy if he was going to see Hendricks on time, but he would call her straight after to ask why she failed to mention she had instructed solicitors. Rob would be unable to receive anything if he was found guilty of murdering Jane, but what claim did Lucy think she had?

CHAPTER SIXTEEN

The lack of a trust fund for Chris occupied Peter's mind during the drive to Hendricks. If the payments Jane made to her brother were voluntary, it suggested Jane had received enough money to make a generous gesture to a brother she rarely saw. And if Lucy and Rob were to be believed, one who continued to be rude and abusive towards her, which didn't make a great deal of sense. Also, unless she were leaving him a large lump sum, it would be in his interests that Jane lived a long and healthy life, so the payments continued.

Another possibility for the regular payments occurred to Peter as he entered the small town of Nettlebridge. Could Chris have been blackmailing Jane for some reason?

So fixated on the financial arrangement between Jane and her brother, Peter hadn't given any thought to what he hoped to gain from speaking to the Walford's family solicitors. Locking his car with only minutes to spare, he accepted he had no choice but to listen to them and play it by ear.

The solicitor, who introduced herself as Veronica, met Peter on time and led him upstairs to a small office. She was older than he had expected but shot up the two flights of stairs and along the winding corridor with surprising speed. The building retained the feeling of the family home it had once been. Once seated, Veronica asked for his official documentation. Peter handed over his card, driver's license and a copy of Lucy's letter instructing them. He waited, holding his breath, fearing it might be rejected.

Veronica barely glanced at the documents before handing them back. "How do you think we can help? It says there that you've been instructed to prove Emily's ex-husband innocent of murdering his recent girlfriend."

Impressed by how quickly she had read Lucy's letter of instruction, Peter asked, "Did Robert Lewis benefit from Emily Walford's will when she died?"

"I repeat, how do you think investigating his first windfall from a deceased partner is going to prove his innocence?"

Peter lamely replied, "I'm interested in discovering the truth."

"Fair enough," Veronica said, leaning back in her chair. "My brother used to work for Walfords back in the day. It was very different when Helen was alive."

"Helen?"

"Emily's grandmother. The company has gone from strength to strength and increased its turnover in recent years but has lost its high regard in the area. Helen was a woman before her time. Her husband may have created the company, but she was its heart and soul. She believed in sharing their good fortune and insisted on good pay for all their workers. She knew everyone who worked for them by name and probably half of their private business. She was the only one who applauded when Emily turned her back on the family."

"Hence her leaving her money to her granddaughter."

"Quite," Veronica said, sitting up straight and turning professional. "What do you want to know?"

"How much money are we talking about? How long before Emily's accident was it bequeathed to her? And whether afterwards, the money went to Rob as her husband, uncontested?"

"Most of Helen's wealth was tied up in the firm, but she left a little over £250,000 to Emily. She would have received it a mere five months before her accident, and it was then passed onto Robert. While I remember mutterings of objections, nobody tried to block the payment." Veronica leaned forward, and directly asked, "If you conclude he had a hand in his girlfriend's death, will you promise to come back and tell me?"

"So far, I have nothing to prove he did," Peter said. "It was the coincidence of the two deaths that struck me, but if I uncover any proof that Rob had a part in either death, I will let you know."

"Thank you," Veronica said, leaning back in her chair. "Did his recent girlfriend inherit a large sum of money before her death?"

"Yes, but not recently. It was several years ago, and it's complicated," Peter said.

"Family finances usually are."

"Do you know the Walford family, personally?"

"Not well, no. Our families lived in the same village, and when I was young, the Walfords were very much part of the community. As their empire has grown, they've distanced themselves. It's all private schools and dining with their own class now. I remember Emily, though. She bucked the trend and would hang out with the local children and drink in the village pub as soon as she was old enough. She reminded me a lot of Helen. I think if she had lived and there had been a family reconciliation, Emily would have been an asset to the company. Her mother was never the same after she died. She was taken by cancer shortly after. I believe her father is still alive and living in a nursing home somewhere. Don't ask me where. Emily's two older brothers run the company now. They may be good businessmen, but they've lost the personal touch."

"Did you see Emily around the time of her accident?"

"No. She had moved away by then. I read about it in the newspapers like everyone else," Veronica said. "I can't tell you anything more about the accident than you could read in the reports, but I've always had my suspicions about her untimely death. I have nothing to substantiate them, but I'm afraid I don't believe in coincidences when there's money involved. It may be nothing more than my jaded view of humanity due to doing this job for too long."

"I understand the sentiment," Peter said. "Do you know if Emily maintained contact with any of her old friends?"

"I believe she cut all ties to follow a more authentic life. Whatever she thought that to be."

"And has there been any contact between the family and Lucy?"

Veronica shook her head sadly. "If Emily's mother had lived

longer, she may have reached out to her daughter. We'll never know now, but the rest of the family is happy to pretend she doesn't exist. Financially, no allowance has ever been made for her."

"Do you know if Rob has ever approached them on Lucy's behalf?"

"The family made it very clear at the time they wanted nothing to do with him or the child, and as far as I know, he stayed away."

Peter stood to shake Veronica's hand. "Thank you for your time. Should I discover anything, I will let you know."

Before standing, Veronica reached into her top desk drawer and pulled out a brown envelope. "I know you said you've requested copies, but you may as well have these now. Helen's and Emily's wills."

CHAPTER SEVENTEEN

Peter flicked through the two wills in his car before heading back. He had enjoyed meeting Veronica, and her information was useful. The money Rob received after Emily's death was substantial, which could explain why he hadn't pressed the family to acknowledge Lucy. He made a mental note to ask how much Lucy knew about her mother's family and whether she might have a financial claim. For most of the journey, he wondered if his failure to accept the coincidence of the two deaths was his own jaded opinion of people.

He let himself into the office and, after an initial panic, successfully disarmed the alarm. He pressed a few buttons on the complicated coffee machine before deciding he would buy a coffee from the shop around the corner if Simon didn't turn up soon. But first, he wanted to speak to Lucy. She answered immediately but said she was at work, so she couldn't speak properly. Peter wanted to meet Lucy's boyfriend to check her alibi, so he arranged to see them at home that evening after they finished work.

He slid out the two wills Veronica had given him and quickly read through them. The inheritance would have been enough for Rob to have bought a good-sized home for himself and Lucy, and he wondered why he hadn't. Discovering where the money went and how much was left would be interesting.

The most obvious assumption was he used it to support himself as a stay-at-home dad, without worrying about what he would do once it ran out. And when it did, he had conveniently met Jane. Or maybe he had a gambling or drug problem back then and had lost it. That would give him something in common with Jane's brother.

Did Chris and Rob know each other before Jane entered the picture? Could Chris have introduced them? It would explain their antagonism and why Chris was so quick to point the finger at Rob when they claimed to barely know one another. While researching Chris, Simon might have stumbled across a connection between the two men.

Peter slid the Walford family's paperwork back inside the envelope. It was the Forbes family's wills he wanted to see. He was still struggling with the bombshell that there was no trust fund. The story Rob had given them about a trust fund had seemed reasonable if Chris had a gambling addiction. Could he assume that was what Jane had told him, and Rob honestly believed that was the situation? And was Chris disinherited solely because of the gambling addiction, or was there more to it? And finally, was it relevant to Jane's murder?

Peter's mind circled the financial implications but kept returning to the same conclusion. Chris would prefer Jane to be alive, unless she had made a generous allowance for him in her will. He was about to head out to the coffee shop when Simon walked in.

"Hi, I'm not late, am I? I thought I was early," Simon said, checking the time. "So, I am. Is the coffee on?" Without waiting for a reply, he shot into the kitchen to set up the coffee machine. "Latte?"

"Yes, please," Peter said, wandering over to watch how the machine was operated. "Have you found out anything about Chris?"

Simon nodded. "There was a long article in the local newspaper about how he was evicted from his home. He must have run up some serious debts as the house was substantial and came with ten acres of land. His parents gave him it as a birthday present, but he remortgaged it and lost the lot.

"I have the reporter's and the local pub owner's names. Both are worth seeing for some more background. Chris wasn't liked by his neighbours; they were pleased to see the back of him. It's not sour grapes with Lucy and Rob. He really is an unpleasant character.

"Also, I've contacted a friend who knows a bit about the gambling world. He's going to make some discreet enquiries about any current gambling debts. Oh, and Jane wasn't a legal secretary but a paralegal. I'm not sure there's much difference in pay, though. More of a status thing." Simon handed Peter a coffee. "Have you found anything interesting?"

Taking his coffee back to his chair, Peter said, "Would you believe there wasn't a trust fund?"

Following him, Simon asked, "What do you mean? No trust fund? That was why Chris visited Jane."

"I won't have a full copy for a week or so, but according to the solicitors, he wasn't mentioned in his parents' will. They left everything to Jane."

"But Lucy and Rob said he regularly pestered Jane for advance payments from the fund," Simon said, putting down his coffee. "Are you sure?"

Peter shrugged. "That's what I was told, even when I queried it. If it's true, Jane was under no legal obligation to give Chris a penny."

"Maybe she felt a moral obligation to share her inheritance. I probably would in her situation," Simon said. "Or he was blackmailing her. If Jane had been giving him money out of the goodness of her heart, he would have been more polite. Lucy and Rob said he was abrasive and abrupt."

Despite having the same suspicion, Peter said, "When they were around. Maybe he behaved differently when they weren't."

"Or it could have been a convenient cover for what they really met up to discuss."

Peter rubbed his face in exasperation. "Which was?"

"I don't know yet."

Peter shook his head. "Either way, unless Jane has left something to Chris, his regular cash source has dried up with her death. It wouldn't be in his interests to murder her."

"True, but that doesn't mean he didn't in a fit of anger, because she didn't give him what he wanted there and then," Simon said stubbornly. "And he might have known she was leaving a lump sum to him on her death."

"Possibly," Peter said. Mulling it over increased his frustration at Foxfields for being so obstructive. "Did you find anything to suggest Chris and Rob knew each other before?"

"Before Rob and Jane got together? No, but then I wasn't looking," Simon said. "Why do you ask?"

"There's the speed at which Chris accused Rob of his sister's murder. How could he be so sure if they only ever saw each other in passing?"

"Good point," Simon said. "How do you think they might have known each other?"

"It's only an idea," Peter admitted. "Despite Rob being left a considerable sum by his first wife, he has nothing to show for it. He doesn't own a home, and his car is ten years old. Maybe he also liked a flutter and lost it that way."

"Or he lived off the money while he stayed home to bring Lucy up," Simon said, determined to defend Rob.

"He could have worked reduced hours as soon as she started school and invested the money in their future to give her some stability. Buying a home would be a good place to start, rather than doing nothing and frittering the money away. He must have realised it would run out sooner or later, and he would be back to square one," Peter said. "That's why I'm wondering if he lost a fair chunk of it gambling."

"You're judging him harshly from a very middle-class point of view," Simon said. "Maybe he believes in social housing and that private ownership is wrong."

"And I think your opinion of him as someone highly principled is rather generous," Peter replied

"Touche. But the truth could be somewhere in the middle," Simon said. "If he wasn't used to handling large sums of money, he wouldn't know the best way to manage it."

"He's savvy enough to have employed a solicitor in relation to Jane's will. As has Lucy. A small detail neither of them volunteered. I'm seeing Lucy and her boyfriend at seven o'clock this evening. Are you free?"

"I'll need to pop home at some point to feed my dogs, but I would like to come. If only to stop you from accusing the poor girl of something," Simon said. "And Rob? You said he has instructed solicitors as well."

"It seems so, but he can wait until later, when I have a feeling that we'll have a long list of questions for him," Peter said. "Do you have an address for Chris?"

"I can't find a registered address for him," Simon replied, knowing he hadn't looked very hard. "I could try a couple of other things to find him."

"Also see if you can get hold of the reporter or the pub landlord you mentioned. They might be able to provide some background information on the family as well. Did you speak to Jane's two work colleagues?"

"Not yet," Simon said, finishing his coffee. "Have you had any lunch? Shall we start with the pub landlord?"

Peter looked up at the clock. "Everywhere will have finished serving lunch by now."

"I'll grab something from the shop along the road, but what about visiting the pub?"

"Ring ahead to check he'll be there. And contact the journalist. We can speak to him afterwards if he also lives out that way. Otherwise, we'll be doing a lot of driving forwards and backwards. Do we know how far from the pub Jane worked? We might be able to interview her colleagues as well."

"All this before seven o'clock," Simon said doubtfully.

"We could split up. One of us interviews the work colleagues while the other speaks to the journalist."

CHAPTER EIGHTEEN

Driving down a steep hill into the village of Tidworth, Simon pointed out a large house set back from the lane. "I think that's where Chris lived. It looks like the one he was standing outside in the news article. There can't be many houses of that style and size in the area."

Peter glanced over and whistled. "If it is, he had some serious debts. On today's prices, that's got to be worth over a million or thereabouts, even without the surrounding land."

The Royal Oak pub was tucked away down a private lane that started a short distance from the village. The unlit, twisty lane would be a trek, and Peter doubted anyone other than dedicated ramblers who walked in heavy rain with their maps inside plastic wallets made the journey on foot. When the car turned the final corner, the pub was obscured by one of the largest oak trees he had ever seen.

"Quite a mystery how the pub got its name," Simon said, pulling into the large car park. "From the number of cars here, it must do a healthy lunchtime trade. I'm starting to worry that I should have booked a table. I assumed it would be dead on weekday afternoons out here in the sticks. The food must be good."

"Hopefully, a decent pint as well," Peter said, climbing out of the car and stretching his back. "Pubs in out-of-the-way places need something to draw customers in to survive."

The front door to the pub was appropriately made of oak. They entered a small lobby area lined by fixed wooden benches. An odd assortment of crockery, plates, cutlery, glasses and beer towels was on the benches. At the far end, there was an honesty box and a small notice inviting customers to help themselves, but a donation for the upkeep of the local church and the village green would be appreciated.

Double doors led from the lobby to a small bar area. In the cramped space, it looked like the three people serving behind the bar were playing a complicated game of Twister as they leaned around one another to reach glasses and beer pumps. Peter and Simon squeezed through a group of men in deep conversation, oblivious to how they blocked access to the bar. Successfully through, they waited in turn to be served.

"What can I get you?"

"We're here to see Henry. Is he around?" Peter asked.

A bearded man pulling a pint, shouted across, "Give them a couple of drinks on the house, and I'll be over in a minute."

By the time they had chosen their drinks and asked for a menu, Henry had finished serving the other customers and walked out from the bar to greet them. After shaking hands, he said, "I've reserved us a table out the back." Looking down at the menus in their hands, he added, "I'm afraid the kitchen is closed. I might be able to persuade the chef to make you something simple if you're quick."

"It's okay. I was just looking," Peter said, returning the menus to the stand.

Henry led them through a labyrinth of alcoves and beamed rooms to a table overlooking the rear garden and gestured for them to sit. "You want to talk about that scoundrel, Chris Forbes?"

"Yes. I don't know if you've heard, but his sister died recently," Simon said.

"Brutally murdered, more like," Henry said. "Of course, we heard. It's been all over the local news. Are you suggesting Chris was involved? The papers say her boyfriend has been arrested."

"We're not suggesting anything," Peter said. "The boyfriend's family has asked us to look at other possibilities, and we're making enquiries about Jane's family."

"Chris is a bully, a liar and a crook. It wouldn't surprise me if he's a murderer as well, but I'm not sure how I can help you. He was barred from here years ago."

"Why was he barred?" Peter asked.

"For being an arrogant arse, upsetting my staff, especially the girls and refusing to settle his bill. He ran up thousands of pounds by intimidating the staff into putting all his drinks and food on a tab he never had. It's still unpaid."

"Not your favourite customer, then," Peter said.

"You could say that," Henry said. "His picture was on the dartboard for a while."

Simon pulled out the newspaper article on the eviction. "You were quoted as saying he was a public menace by the local press."

Henry looked at the article and laughed. "Because of his family and his big house, he thought he was a cut above everyone else. He acted like he was lord of the manor. Seeing him evicted was one of the best days of my life. Sad for the family, though. That house had been in the family for generations. His grandfather, who lived there before him, was a true gentleman. Always polite and generous, whereas Chris was a pig of a man. I can't tell you how happy I was to see the back of him, even though it left me out of pocket."

"He came from a wealthy family?" Peter asked.

"They were. Riches to rags in three generations. I think that's the saying. The people who eventually bought the house had to pay a fortune to put it right because it was in such a neglected state. They bought it for a pittance, so I suppose it's all swings and roundabouts if you have the cash."

"The land alone must be worth a fair bit," Simon said.

"Ah. He somehow managed to hang on to most of it. It's where he lives now. They initially tried to buy the land to get rid of him but gave up. He's not so high and mighty now that he's living in a makeshift hovel. He rarely dares show his face around the village these days."

"We've been trying to find a registered address for him," Simon said. "Could you tell us where he lives?"

"That'll be because it's not a registered address. He's not

supposed to be living there, but he does."

"How do we find it?"

Henry stood. "It's probably easier if I draw you a map. Do you want another couple of pints?"

Peter nodded. "But we'll pay for them."

While Peter and Simon drank their fresh drinks, Henry talked as he started to draw. "Chris insists the place is stables and barns for the handful of ponies he bought, and he only uses the area furnished as a home when he's taking a break between caring for them. Nonsense, but so far, he has gotten away with it. Do you know where he used to live?"

"The large house on the hill before the road drops down into the village?" Simon queried.

"Correct," Henry said, pointing to his drawn map. "When you leave the village, turn right onto the single-lane track below the house. The stone walls have collapsed in several places, so you'll see you're driving the length of three large paddocks. Keep going until you reach the edge of the woods. There's a layby on your left. I would leave your car there if I were you unless you're in a four-wheel drive. You'll see a muddy track with a handful of chippings thrown down heading into the trees. Walk along there, and around the first bend, and you'll come to two stable blocks. The one on the left is where he lives. There's a good chance he'll be slumped in front of the racing on the TV. What mood he'll be in is anyone's guess."

"Did he have a major falling out with his parents before they died?" Peter asked.

"He lost the house the family had owned for generations! They never spoke to him again. Some say it's what finished them off."

"Did you know his sister, Jane?" Peter asked.

"I used to when she was younger and still lived at home. She was nothing like her brother," Henry said. "She was shy and awkward. If I remember rightly, she was bullied at boarding school and by the local kids when she came home. I always felt a little sorry for her."

"When would you have seen her last?"

"A fair few years ago. She lived with her parents right up to when they died, but she didn't go out much. I have no idea what she did with her time or whether she had friends. She sold up as soon as she inherited the house. Rumour was that she didn't have any choice once all the debts were paid, but as she didn't talk to people much, I can't confirm whether that's true or not."

"Is there anyone else in the village who knew her better?" Simon asked.

Henry shook his head. "Like I said, she didn't mix much. Lonely old existence, but there you go. Money isn't everything. If that's everything, I should get back to the bar."

Peter thanked Henry and handed him his card before he left the table. Over their drinks, Peter and Simon decided to quickly speak with Jane's work colleagues as previously arranged, and afterwards drive back to talk to Chris. The journalist could wait for another day.

CHAPTER NINETEEN

The firm Jane worked for was a small affair on the edge of a modern retail park. While geographically, it wasn't far from her childhood home, it was worlds apart in style. Parking the car in front of the glass-fronted building, Simon said, "Why on earth didn't Chris meet his sister here? It's far closer."

"Maybe he did," Peter said. "Or possibly she asked him not to bother her at work."

Simon opened the door into an open-plan office space with only two desks occupied. The brunette closest to the door sprung from her chair. "Hello, you must be Simon and Peter. I'm Caron."

The dark-haired girl, still seated, gave them a girlish wave. "Hi, I'm Clemmie."

"The bosses are out, so we have the place to ourselves," Caron said, sounding like a naughty schoolgirl. "We can put up the closed sign and talk in the conference room."

"I'll make the coffee," Clemmie said.

Clemmie and Caron told them what little they knew about Jane, like a well-versed double act.

"She moaned occasionally about Rob drinking and Lucy being untidy, but I don't think either issue was a big problem," Caron offered.

"She told me that before meeting Rob, she had been single for several years," Clemmie added.

"Were you surprised when she decided to study to become a paralegal?" Simon asked.

"I was," Caron said. "She wasn't particularly ambitious."

"But she was hardworking, cheerful and a good team player,"

Clemmie said. "Why shouldn't she try to better herself."

"Can you think of anyone who might have wanted to harm Jane?" Simon asked.

"No, but to be fair, we rarely socialised out of work other than for the occasional birthday and the office Christmas do."

"Did Jane ever meet up with anyone after work or during her lunch hour?" Simon asked.

"Not that I ever saw," Caron said. "Are you saying she had a secret lover?"

"We were thinking more along the lines of a brother."

"I didn't know she had a brother," Caron said. "Clemmie?"

"She never talked about her family or having a brother."

"Would you be surprised if I said she came from a local, wealthy family?"

"Yes," Caron said, looking surprised. "Which one?"

"But she was so ordinary," Clemmie said.

Listening in, a picture of an intensely private person telling people only what she wanted them to know formed in Peter's mind. There was generally a good reason why people kept aspects of their lives so secret. "You told the police Jane left work early the day she was killed. Do you know where she was going?"

"She took the whole afternoon off," Clemmie said. "She left at lunchtime."

"She was going shopping, and then she had an appointment with her solicitors," Caron said.

"She didn't mention visiting solicitors to me," Clemmie said. "She said something about buying an outfit for an evening meal. Rob was taking her out that evening. I've thought about it since speaking to the police, and I think she was nervous about it."

"Any idea why?" Peter asked.

"No, it was just a vague feeling I had," Clemmie said. "Maybe she was going to tell him something."

"Do you think she was pregnant?" Caron asked.

Clemmie pulled a face before saying, "At her age?"

"I can confirm she wasn't pregnant," Peter said. "Do you know the name of the person or the firm of solicitors she had an appointment with or what it was about?"

"No, sorry."

Peter thanked them and ended the interview, asking them to contact him if they later remembered anything else that might be useful to their investigation.

Walking to the car, Simon said, "Strange they knew so little about Jane's past. According to Rob, they were her closest friends."

"It's more interesting how she seems to have reinvented herself in a few short years after her parent's death. A hardworking team player is miles away from a socially awkward girl who rarely spoke," Peter said, climbing into the car. "And it begs the question, what was she so secretive about?"

"A difficult childhood? Bullying leaves deep scars," Simon said, settling in the car seat.

"Maybe," Peter said. "I want to make a quick call about her visiting her solicitors the afternoon of her death, before we look for Chris."

He was put through to the same woman he had spoken to previously at Foxfields solicitors. Under the guise of client confidentiality, she wouldn't confirm whether Jane had an appointment that afternoon, let alone what they discussed. When the call ended, Peter threw his phone on the dashboard. "I don't understand why they're being so obstructive."

"Most people only visit solicitors if they are making a major life change. Do you think she was discussing a change in her financial arrangement with Chris?" Simon asked.

"Possibly, but true to form, they're refusing to say anything," Peter said. "Come on. Let's see if her brother can shed any light on her intentions."

CHAPTER TWENTY

If it hadn't been for Henry's map, Simon would have driven past the single-track lane without realising it was there. Even if he had spotted it, he would have assumed it was a private drive or a farm access. Simon did his best to avoid the potholes and clumps of mud from tractor tyres as they wound their way to the layby.

Luckily, the weather had been dry and sunny for the past few weeks, or the rutted track through the trees would have been a quagmire. After a short but steep walk, they came to an old truck parked on a concrete yard between two low wooden buildings. The one on the right was clearly a stable block, while the one on the left looked more like a storage barn than a home. Beyond the buildings, they could see five or six ponies grazing.

As they walked closer, two black Alsatians appeared snarling and growling, stopping Peter and Simon in their tracks.

Peter took a couple of steps back. "Henry didn't mention anything about guard dogs. We should go back and see if he has a mobile number for Chris."

Standing his ground, Simon said, "I don't like the look of them either, but let's see if Chris comes out. He must be able to hear them."

Continuing to walk backwards, Peter said, "We've already lost the element of surprise. I think we need to get out of here. We can regroup in the pub and try to find his phone number."

The door to the barn slammed open, and a man holding a shotgun stepped out. "Who the hell are you?" Despite the warmth of the afternoon, he wore a woollen jumper over a checked flannel shirt and a flat cap. While dated, his clothes were of a quality not seen in high street chain stores.

Shouting over the growling dogs, Simon said, "We're investigating the death of your sister."

"Working for the police, are you?"

Without answering the question, Simon said, "We wanted a quick word about her relationship with Rob Lewis and his daughter Lucy."

"Could you call the dogs back?" Peter asked, with a slight squeak in his voice.

"Get back here," Chris growled in a tone as low as the dogs'. As the dogs walked back to the side of the building and flopped down, Chris lowered his gun, and grunted, "What do you want to know?"

"A little more background information," Simon called. "Something definitive to connect Rob to the murder, otherwise he'll walk."

"You'd best come in. Don't pet the dogs on your way past if you like your hands where they are at the end of your arms."

Peter scuttled warily past the dogs as he followed Simon and Chris through the doorway, closing the door behind him. A small boot room jammed with wellingtons and coats led into a room with a sofa, armchair, coffee table, and a large-screen television on the wall. The floor was rough concrete, and there was no effort to soften it with rugs. Peter could see a fully equipped kitchen through an open door at the end of the room.

Chris turned the volume down on a horse race that was showing but continued to watch it. Over his shoulder, he asked, "Do you want a drink?"

Peter eyed an expensive bottle of whisky and a half-full tumbler on the table. Despite his untidy appearance it would be easy to assume Chris was eccentric rather than broke from his posh accent and air of entitled arrogance. "Not for me, thank you."

"I'm good," Simon said.

Chris stood watching the end of the race on the screen with an impenetrable expression before dropping heavily into the armchair. "What do you want?"

Sitting next to Simon on the low sofa, Peter said, "You're very sure that Rob was responsible for your sister's death. Could you tell us why that is?"

Chris drank from his whisky glass before replying, "It's obvious, isn't it? For the money. He never loved her. It was all about the money. He was just waiting for her to change her will in his favour. Once she did, she was writing her death sentence. I warned her this would happen, but would she listen?"

"Did she recently change the terms of her will?" Peter asked.

"I think she did, but I'm not even entitled to a copy, even though by rights, half of the money is mine," Chris said, bitterness dripping from every word. "Daylight robbery is what it is."

"What money would that be?" Peter asked.

"From our parents. By rights, it belonged to both of us."

"Are you in direct contact with Foxfields Solicitors?"

Chris shook his head. "That slippery bunch of crooks. Dealing with them is like trying to get blood out of a stone."

Recognising the description, Peter asked, "Were you told that she recently changed her will?"

"No, but it stands to reason, doesn't it? That's why I can't have a copy. While that snake oil salesman gets the lot. I don't trust that daughter of his, either. Common little chav thinks she's better than the likes of me. There was no saving Jane once they got their claws into her."

"Were you and your sister close?" Peter asked.

"Close enough before *they* came on the scene. I didn't see her so much then. That's what parasites do. They isolate their victim from their family." Chris paused to sip from his glass. "I've made some bad choices in the past. I expect you already know all about that. But Jane was the only family I had. Her death has hit me hard."

"Before Jane started dating Rob, did you see each other regularly?" Peter asked.

"We would keep in touch." Chris drank some more whisky. "If I had known she would be taken away from me so soon, I would have made more of an effort. I would have been a better brother, but it's too late now."

Peter thought Chris was exaggerating his brotherly care, but his grief was real. "Would it be fair to say you saw much more of your sister before she met Rob?" When Chris nodded and mumbled something inaudible, he asked, "Was seeing less of her a gradual process, or did it happen suddenly?"

Chris topped up his whisky glass. "Over time, he wormed his way in and then started to control her. That's what happened. That's how people like him operate. Subtle, so their victim doesn't realise what is happening."

"That must have been very upsetting, especially as Jane was your only sibling."

"Yes, it was," Chris replied eagerly.

"We understand that shortly before her death, your only contact was to discuss a financial matter between you," Peter said. "What was the agreement?"

"That was a private family matter and nobody else's business."

"Unfortunately, with a murder investigation, nothing remains private," Peter said. "Why was your sister giving you money?"

"It was my money." Chris put down his tumbler and threw his hands up in frustration. "It belonged to my parents. It was left solely to Jane for complicated tax reasons, but it was always considered our money."

Peter studied Chris, questioning whether he really believed that tax was the only reason his parents hadn't mentioned him in their wills. "Why didn't she give you a lump sum after she inherited?"

"It was tied up in investment funds. Tax again. I don't know. Neither of us had children or any health concerns. It was something we always intended to sort out at some stage, but we didn't have any sense of urgency. That's why he killed her," Chris said, his tone turning bitter. "To get his grubby little hands on all the money."

"Did Jane tell you that she was having a will drawn up?" Simon asked.

Chris shrugged and topped up his whisky. "It's what happens. You see it all the time in the news. Gullible women being taken advantage of."

"And you think that was what Rob was doing?" Simon asked.

"Not think. I know."

"How do you know? And what was he doing?" Simon pressed.

"Controlling her mind. Pretending to be in love with her when he wasn't."

"What makes you think that was what he was doing?"

Chris shrugged and lifted his glass. "Stuff."

Peter waited for Chris to put his glass down and asked, "Before her death, did you think Rob would physically harm her?"

"No, of course not. If I thought that, I would have stepped in," Chris said. "That's why I feel so guilty. She was my little sister, and I should have protected her. Now, the least I can do is see him punished for what he did."

"But you never had any concerns about the relationship before? You didn't see any signs of violence?" Peter asked.

"I had concerns over the way he was controlling her, but no, I never saw any signs of physical violence. But that doesn't mean there wasn't any, just that I wasn't close enough to see anything. He made sure I was kept away from her. He kept her isolated."

"Did you know Rob before he met your sister?" Peter asked.

"No, and if I knew who introduced them, I would … Well, I wouldn't be happy about it."

"Okay, I understand," Peter said. "You've said Jane changed after meeting Rob. Can you think of anyone else who would have noticed this change?"

"Her friends, maybe. I wouldn't describe either of us as extroverts with a wide circle of friends. But there might be someone."

"Do you know the names of her friends?"

"No," Chris sulkily admitted.

"We understand you've contacted the solicitors about Jane's will."

"Foxfields solicitors called me. I only replied to try to prevent *him* from benefitting from her murder. If I'm successful, I will suggest they give the money to charity."

"That's very generous of you." Peter looked up at the television where another horse race was about to start. "You like the horses?"

"The sport of kings. I do, and yes, I enjoy a flutter every now and again when I can afford it."

"And when you can't afford it?"

"I've admitted my past mistakes and learned my lesson."

"Do you currently owe anyone any money?"

Chris looked away towards the screen, and asked, "Would you lend me money?"

"Probably not, but that doesn't answer my question," Peter said.

Focussed on the TV screen, Chris muttered, "The answer is no."

"What was your sister like?" Peter asked. "Before she met Rob?"

"Annoying, like most little sisters. Always being clumsy and putting her foot in it," Chris said, smiling to himself. The smile disappeared, and he added, "She was kind and generous, but naïve. She didn't understand men like Rob. She couldn't see that he latched onto her for her money. He was manipulating her from the start."

"You never thought he loved her for herself?"

"Never."

"Even though you didn't socialise with them?"

"I saw enough to know."

"Before we go, I'm afraid I have to ask where you were the night your sister was killed," Peter said. "The report mentions an emergency vet visit."

"One of the ponies, Bobbie, had a bad bout of colic. So bad I had to call the vet out."

"Roughly what time was that?"

"About eight o'clock. I spotted something wrong when I completed my evening check. They were still coming in at night then."

"What time did the vet leave?"

"Sometime after ten, but I stayed with Bobbie until the early hours. Even then, I came out a couple of times to check on her. I couldn't sleep with the worry."

"But you were alone after ten?"

"I was with Bobbie and the dogs," Chris snapped. "I would never leave a colicky horse. You can ask anyone that, and they'll all say the same. Unlike some, I take good care of my animals."

"Okay. Thank you for your time," Peter said. "I think we have enough to be going on with, but we might want to chat with you again."

"I'll give you any help you need to put that monster away behind bars," Chris said. "And sorry about earlier when you arrived. I didn't know who you were, and you can't be too careful living out here alone like I do."

Walking along the track to the car, Simon asked, "Why didn't you push him more on where he was that night and why he was so certain Rob wasn't in love with Jane?"

"Apart from the fact it was getting us nowhere, and I didn't want him becoming suspicious about who we were? You saw his shotgun and dogs, the same as I did. I didn't think antagonising him out in the middle of nowhere when he had been drinking was a great idea. I pushed him as hard as I dare," Peter said. "You have animals. Would you say his are well cared for?"

"From what I could see, they seemed happy and well-fed, but that doesn't mean he kept an all-night vigil over the pony like he said."

"I'll ring the vet when we get back," Peter said. "What did you think of him? Could he be right when he says Rob isolated Jane? We've commented on her lack of close friends."

"All Chris cares about is getting his hands on his sister's money," Simon replied. "Lucy is a pleasant, well-adjusted girl. Would that be the case if her father was a crazed narcissist?"

"Fair point," Peter conceded.

"What did you make of him?"

"He's not someone to warm to, and I'm sure he was lying when he said he had no current debts, but I think his grief is real," Peter said.

"Or his guilt," Simon said.

Peter scratched the back of his head, "The only thing I know for sure is that we need to see a copy of Jane's previous and final wills. Chris seemed strangely confident that she intended to amend it to leave her money to Rob. Although, I don't know how much of anything he said wasn't his drink-fuelled imagination."

"And his motive for murder," Simon said.

When they reached the car, Peter pulled out his pen and jotted down the old truck's registration number, which he had memorised. "There are no cameras near where Jane lived, but it would be interesting to check the main routes between her home and here to see if his truck pops up in the area."

"That would answer the question, one way or the other," Simon said, starting the car engine.

"Assuming we can get hold of the footage," Peter said. "I'll contact the police and ask once we're back at the office."

"If I'm going to feed and walk my dogs before visiting Lucy, I'll need to head home after I drop you off," Simon said.

"I'll ring Lucy to see if we can put it back an hour and I'll pick you up from home to save you some time," Peter said.

CHAPTER TWENTY-ONE

Peter was taken aback when he pulled into the drive of Holly Bush Farm. Charlie had said Simon was wealthy with a large farmhouse, but the place looked more like a grand manor house than a farm. He guessed it had at least eight bedrooms, and he knew Charlie had a separate flat in one of the outbuildings. The surrounding land and the house looked perfectly maintained, which wouldn't be a cheap undertaking. Simon came out the front door, eating a packet of crisps before Peter stopped the car.

Simon offered a crisp to Peter as he climbed in the passenger seat. "Perfect timing. I like to have the dogs settled before I come out. It sets them off if someone knocks on the door. Do you have pets? What are their names? I forgot to ask before."

"A stray cat moved in with me for a few years but then wandered off again," Peter said, turning the car around. "My daughter is always trying to persuade me to get a kitten. Apparently, it would give my life more meaning."

"Well-meaning family and friends," Simon said, rolling his eyes. "They can be a nightmare, can't they? But she's right. All pets are great, but dogs are best. I couldn't be without mine. We have a couple of cats, but they mostly live out in the barns. If I hear of any kittens going, I'll be sure to give you a shout."

"Please don't. I'm fine, thanks," Peter said. "I'm not at home enough, so it wouldn't be fair."

"But that's the beauty of cats if you can't have a dog. They're very independent."

"They still need someone around to feed them and clean up

after them."

"You do like animals, don't you?" Simon asked. "I don't trust people who don't like animals. Even Charlie has come around to the idea."

Avoiding the question, Peter said, "You're going to have to change your tune about Chris, then. I spoke to his vet earlier, and Chris does take good care of his animals. They wouldn't be surprised if he did spend all night with that pony. On your reasoning, maybe he's innocent after all."

"It doesn't quite work like that. I don't trust people who don't like animals, but that doesn't mean I trust everyone who does. There are good and bad animal owners."

"If we rely on the vet's word, Chris is one of the good ones."

"But is he a good payer?"

Peter laughed, noting again how Simon could be so astute under all his drivel. "They've had a few problems with payment of bills, but more interestingly, Jane has settled some of them in the past. Including some very expensive colic surgery a year ago for the said Bonnie."

"Bobbie," Simon said. "The pony is called Bobbie."

"A minor detail."

"On the contrary," Simon said. "You're really not an animal person, are you? Mistaking a pet's name is a major issue for a loving owner."

"If you say so," Peter said dismissively.

"It's possible that Chris visited his sister that night to say another vet's bill was on the way, and she refused to pay it."

"He viciously attacked her over a vet's bill. I know how emotional people are about their animals, but that's a stretch," Peter said.

"It's a possibility."

Simon continued to sing the praises of pet ownership while Peter tried to ignore him for the rest of the journey. By the time they arrived outside Lucy's boyfriend's house, Peter was starting to understand why Charlie found Simon so infuriating. He was giving him a headache.

CHAPTER TWENTY-TWO

Jake's home was a small, red-bricked terrace with a front garden of dumped rubbish and a tangle of weeds. After a short delay, Lucy threw open the door with a wide smile and called them in. They climbed over bicycles, shoes and boxes to reach a small, dimly lit kitchen. A cookery book was propped open, and a curry was bubbling away in a pan on the stove. Stirring the concoction, Lucy said, "Sit down. Can I get you something to drink?"

Peter looked over at the sink overflowing with dirty crockery and declined. Nodding towards the simmering saucepan, he asked, "Is it something you can turn down and leave to its own devices for half an hour?"

Lucy stirred the pot, turned the hob down, and threw the spoon into the pile in the sink. "That sounds serious. Have you discovered something?"

"We would like to know about Jane's will and the solicitors you've instructed to protect your interests," Peter said. "Do you have a copy of it?"

Lucy fussed around the counter before pulling out a kitchen chair and sitting on it cross-legged. "Oh, that. I had almost forgotten about it. I instructed the solicitors because I received a letter saying I should. I've since realised I don't need them. I remember something about Chris contesting the will because he's convinced Dad is guilty. I'm guessing I was mentioned as a beneficiary should Dad die at the same time. As Dad is innocent, the whole thing is academic. When I get around to it, I'll tell them that I no longer need them."

"Have you a copy of the letter?"

"Which letter?" Lucy asked with wide-eyed innocence.

"The letter advising you to seek legal representation," Peter said with forced patience, not taken in by the scatty pretence.

Lucy shrugged. "I probably threw it out. Sorry, I'm not good with paperwork, and like I said, I didn't think it was important."

"And the will?" Peter asked, convinced Lucy was lying. People don't dismiss the possibility of receiving an inheritance. Families fall out over wills all the time.

"I don't remember seeing one. It was all legal jargon that I didn't understand. If there was a copy, it's probably in the bin as well."

A bare-chested man in low-slung jeans walked in. "Hey, that smells good. When will it be ready?" he asked as he pulled a beer can from the fridge.

"When our guests leave, Jake," Lucy replied, giving him a stern look.

"Oh, yeah. Hi. I'll go and watch the box while you're talking."

Peter turned in his chair. "We want to talk to you as well. Why don't you join us?"

Jake took a slurp of beer and burped loudly. "I'll go and find a T-shirt."

Lucy squirmed, looking embarrassed, while Jake scratched his chest and burped again before leaving. "I wish he wouldn't do that."

"Are you happy staying here?" Simon asked, looking overly concerned.

"Of course. Jake will be different when he comes down. He's always a bit of a slob when he gets home from work. By mid-evening, he's almost human," Lucy joked. "Anyway, it won't be for long. I'll be living back with Dad soon. Have you seen him? How was he?"

"Yes, and he was good," Simon said.

"Sorry to interrupt," Peter said. "But did the solicitor say how much money Jane was leaving in her will?"

"No. Like I said, I was told to contact one out of the blue. I didn't really understand why. It was something about provisions for this and that, so I didn't pay it any attention. I do that when it's something irrelevant. That makes me sound awful. What I mean is, I'm not interested in her money. It would go against all my principles. I've never agreed with inherited wealth. I'm only concerned about Dad and how he's coping."

"Did your dad talk to you about your mother's family?" Peter asked.

"Just that we were better off without them," Lucy said. "I've never met them or have any idea where they live."

"How did you get along with Jane?" Peter asked, still not entirely convinced by Lucy's disinterest.

"Umm, very well. She was fun, and she made Dad happy. If he was away working, we often had a girl's night in together. I miss her being around," Lucy said sadly. "It must be far worse for Dad. And on top of that, to be accused of her murder is unthinkable. I don't know what more I can say to convince you that they were a normal, happy couple and Dad would never hurt her."

"And you accepted the part she had in your dad's life?" Peter asked.

"It's not like I'm a child. I have my own life to lead. It was good to know that he had someone special."

"How about Jake? How did he get along with Jane?" Simon asked.

"They never properly met. He was shocked when I told him what happened, but he didn't really know her."

"Had he seen more of your dad?" Simon asked.

"No, not really. We haven't been together that long. We're a long way from him asking for my hand in marriage," Lucy tried to joke, but it fell flat.

"When we first met, you suggested Chris offered you a place to stay," Peter said. "Do you know where he had in mind?"

"Did I say that? He tried to be all nice to me and said we should stick together - rubbish like that. I honestly can't remember whether he actually offered me somewhere to stay. He might have done, I suppose," Lucy said vaguely.

Jake walked back in, wearing a baggy T-shirt, wafting off aftershave and looking much brighter than when he had left. "What's going on?"

"We're talking about Dad and Jane, and somehow got onto Chris," Lucy said.

Slumping into the last chair, Jake asked, "Are you going to sort things for her old man?"

"We're trying to find out who killed Jane, if that's what you mean," Simon said. "Where were you that night?"

"I was here waiting for Luce to come over," Jake said. "Wasn't I, Hun?"

"Yes," Lucy said, taking his hand. "I arrived on time for once."

"What did you do that evening?" Peter asked.

"We had a quiet night in," Lucy said.

"I hadn't seen Luce all week," Jake said. "I'm sure you don't need a blow-by-blow account of how we spent the evening."

Simon stiffly said, "All we need is confirmation that you were here together all night."

"We sure were," Jake said, wrapping an arm around Lucy.

"But only you two can confirm that," Peter said.

"Threesomes aren't our thing," Jake said, getting up to retrieve another beer can from the fridge.

"The night Jane was killed, did your father call you?" Peter asked.

Lucy blushed before giving Peter a coy smile. "We were occupied at the time. Dad sounded drunk, and I couldn't work out what he was saying. I thought it was a pocket call and hung up."

Jake returned to the table and draped an arm over Lucy. "Yeah, I remember that."

"How did you get on with Jane and Rob?" Simon asked Jake.

Jake laughed and slurped his beer. "He doesn't think I'm good enough for Luce."

"He's never said that," Lucy protested.

"He didn't have to," Jake replied. "No worries, I'm used to it. A lot of people outside my field look down on me. People who don't know what I'm earning, anyway."

"What do you do?"

"I'm a computer analyst and a bit of an SEO expert. I do well enough."

Lucy stood. "Can I check on the food? I think it might be ready."

"Sure. We'll leave you to your meal," Peter said.

Simon stood up. "We'll keep in touch. Please try not to worry about your dad."

During the journey home, Simon expressed his dislike of Jake and disbelief that Lucy saw anything in him. Peter kept quiet, wondering how much Jake earned. He had heard people could earn eye-watering amounts of money if they were good in those fields. If he were, would it completely negate any financial reason for them harming Jane if Lucy was a named beneficiary in her will? And did she really know nothing about her mother's family? She must have been curious at some point growing up.

Peter briefly tuned into Simon, who was questioning why if Jake was earning such good money, he was living in a dump. Peter knew from his daughter how hard it was for young people to own any property because of the spiralling values, and Jake didn't strike him as someone likely to be house-proud. He tuned out from Simon's ramblings, looking forward to dropping Simon off and having a peaceful evening at home, pondering whether Lucy was as innocent and altruistic as she claimed.

CHAPTER TWENTY-THREE

Peter groaned when he turned the corner to see Dick's dilapidated camper van parked outside his cottage. He was fond of Dick and Gladys, but dealing with them took reserves of energy he didn't currently have. After a day of listening to Simon, he was tired and wanted to grab something to eat before relaxing for the remainder of the evening. Wearily, he parked behind the van blocking his drive and opened his garden gate.

Gladys appeared out of the fading light and air kissed Peter on both cheeks. "There you are, you dirty stop-out. I've been waiting for you. Where have you been? You weren't in the pub, I checked. Do you have a new woman you haven't told me about, you sly old fox?"

"Less of the old," Peter said, sensing his quiet evening slip away as Gladys closely followed him to the front door. He inserted his key in the lock. "Why don't you come in."

"Thank you I will, but just for a while," Gladys said as she bustled past Peter and into the kitchen. "Shall I put the kettle on?"

"Go ahead, as you're already halfway there," Peter said. "Where's Dick?"

"Oh, the poor pet. He's not with me. That's why I've come over alone."

Peter dropped heavily to his chair. "What's happened? Nothing serious, I hope."

"It's the end of the world as far as my dear Dick is concerned. Where's the sugar? It's not where it usually is."

Peter pointed. "Over there, in that jar that says sugar on the side."

"Oh, yes, of course. Silly me. I think it's gotten to me, as well. She was such a dear, gentle thing. As soon as we've drunk our coffee, I'll have to get straight back to him. Shall I put a shot of something in? Brandy, whisky?"

Rubbing his face, Peter said, "If you like. You know where I keep it, but what has happened?"

Gladys shot out of the kitchen to the drink cabinet in the snug, shouting, "I'll tell you when I get back." She reappeared moments later with a bottle of brandy. She made the coffee, added a generous measure of alcohol and carried the mugs to the table. "This is cosy, isn't it? We haven't sat together like this around your table for weeks."

"Lovely," Peter said, taking a sip of coffee. "Now, what's happened?"

"It's Colin. She had another of her turns this afternoon. She turned sixteen only last week, and they've become a regular occurrence. Only this time, she didn't recover. We waited and waited but had no choice other than to take her to the vet. We were both there when she was put to sleep. Dick is beyond himself with grief. He loved that dog. I think more than he loves me, sometimes." Gladys paused briefly to sip her coffee. "So, I have some bad news for you. With things as they are, we won't be ballroom dancing this week."

Relieved he didn't have to think of an excuse for why he couldn't join them for their weekly dance session, Peter pulled a sad face, and said, "That's a shame, but I perfectly understand."

"I knew you would, but I wanted to tell you in person."

"Well, now you've given me your sad news, don't hang around on my behalf. I'm sure Dick will be missing you," Peter said, rekindling his hopes for a relaxing evening.

"If I'm perfectly honest, much as I loved Colin, I could do with a break from all his lamenting. Dick, bless his soul, is being very dramatic and demanding." Gladys gave a winning smile and settled back to enjoy her coffee. "I have known loss and sadness all my life, so I find it easier to deal with. Colin was a dear old girl, but they all break your heart in the end. It's a sad fact that we live longer than our beloved pets. All you can do is give them the best life possible and accept it when they go. I made the mistake of suggesting we look for a puppy. Dick reacted as if I had just suggested we should roast Colin for supper. That's when I decided it would be a good time to call on my dear friend Peter to check he was doing okay." Gladys paused to pat Peter's hand. "Are you doing okay?"

Peter nodded with a weak smile and looked out the window. "I didn't think Dick allowed anyone to drive his campervan."

"He doesn't know."

"I trust you're insured to drive it?"

"I suppose I should do my duty and return to support Dick through his hour of need. Although it's already been much longer than an hour," Gladys said, staring glumly at her mug. "Oh! Before I go. I heard we have a mutual friend. Simon Morris."

"You know Simon?" Peter asked. He didn't know why he was surprised when Gladys and Dick tended to know everyone, and they were all as bonkers as one another.

"Yes. I've known him since he was a teenager. He used to be a good polo player," Gladys said. "Between you and me, he looked rather fetching in his britches."

Peter nearly spat out a mouthful of coffee at the vision of Gladys lusting after Simon in tight jodhpurs and leather boots. He couldn't imagine Simon on a horse, but then he thought back to his home. Polo was the sport of the privileged rich. Who else could afford a string of highly trained horses to bat a ball around a football pitch?

"Of course, that was before. He's changed since those days. He was quite wild back then," Gladys said. "Well, I must get going."

"Before what?" Peter couldn't resist asking, although he knew that he might regret it. It could be a long story.

"Before you know."

"I don't know. That's why I'm asking," Peter said. "Before what?"

Gladys resettled herself in the chair. "I'll make it quick as you are quite correct. I should get back in case my darling Dick needs me. A few years ago, I can't remember how many now, Simon's sister and parents were killed in a bomb blast at a concert."

Peter felt a shiver go down his spine and put down his mug. That was the last thing he was expecting to hear. "That's terrible."

"Poor Simon. It took everyone by surprise," Gladys said, shaking her head. "After the funeral, he disappeared for months. He said he was travelling the world to get his head straight, but I always thought there was more to it. Anyway, when he returned, he had Kate in tow. She seems to have calmed and turned him around. Mind you, she's had heartbreak in her life. Her first husband was killed in a car crash. Don't you think that's terribly sad?"

Peter's head spun with the new information, and all he managed was a nod. On top of the shock, he was angry that Charlie hadn't mentioned it. He remembered Fiona telling him that Simon was a very private person. Maybe that was why Charlie didn't say anything. He realised Gladys was still speaking, so he tuned back in.

"I think they were drawn together by a magical force we can't see. Two distraught, lost souls searching for each other in the darkness. It was the same for me and Dick. We were meant to be, which is why he was drawn to this area when he could have wandered anywhere. That was always his plan, to keep driving wherever the campervan took him. But it ended up parked in my garage. These things can't be random. On that note, I really must get going. Toodle pip."

Peter listened to Gladys crunching through the gears as she drove away. Life was incredibly cruel sometimes. Feeling too shaken and drained to cook an evening meal, he made cheese on toast and carried it to his snug. He settled into his favourite chair to eat it while still making sense of Simon's history. His last thought was he would be more indulgent of Simon prattling on about animals, unsuitable boyfriends and where to have lunch before he fell asleep.

CHAPTER TWENTY-FOUR

When Peter woke up the following morning in the armchair, he realised they hadn't agreed on firm plans for the day or when they would meet up in the office. He sighed when he looked at his pile of notes from the other night on the table. They weren't any closer to proving Rob's innocence.

If anything, he had been moving in the opposite direction. On top of Rob having argued with Jane and having no credible alibi at the time of her death, he was possibly going to benefit financially. Just as he'd done after his first wife's death. If Chris was to be believed, Rob had been slowly isolating Jane from her friends in preparation for her murder.

Due to Jane's secrecy, they knew very little about her. There was nothing to point to why she had been murdered in anything other than a domestic argument other than a possible change to her will.

Her transformation from an ungainly, bullied child to a friendly and very ordinary work colleague intrigued Peter. It also contradicted Chris's claim that Rob was making her more withdrawn. Her promotional work photograph showed an attractive, confident-looking woman - a million miles away from a gawky teenager. Having made the transition once, he doubted that she would allow herself to be dominated and belittled so easily by Rob, even if that was his intention.

Chris had an obvious motive for pointing the finger of blame at Rob. He hoped he would receive Jane's money if Rob was found guilty of her murder, but he couldn't discount his drunken accusations and say he had no grounds for any of his allegations against Rob.

The pub landlord suggested that Jane was forced to sell the family home for financial reasons, but that might be nothing more than speculation. Little about Chris made any sense if there was no family money to inherit. Chris was an unstable character without a good alibi, but until a copy of Jane's final will was released, he couldn't ascertain whether he was a credible alternative suspect. If there wasn't a pot of gold and he wasn't a beneficiary, then Jane's death ran contrary to his interests, and he seemed genuinely upset by her death. Only if he had been a beneficiary but was about to be written out in favour of Rob, did he have something to gain.

The vet had already treated the pony. Would Chris have left the sick pony in the middle of the night to drive to his sister's home, to ask her to pay a bill he wouldn't receive for at least a couple of days? Peter thought it was unlikely, but he made a note to remind himself to chase the police for camera footage. If his truck had been picked up by any cameras that night, he had some explaining to do.

The answer to his central question was in the will that Jane's solicitors were refusing to release. His growing frustration with the solicitors made him grind his teeth. He doubted they'd had a change of heart overnight, but he checked his e-mails anyway. As he expected, they hadn't.

Over breakfast, his thoughts strayed to Simon and his past. Simon's sharp mind had struck him from the first day. Although his astute observations often sat beside mundane ramblings about irrelevant subjects, he thought Charlie's assessment of him as lazy and work-shy was wrong. He wondered where the desire to become a private investigator came from. Did he choose to probe other people's lives to block out thoughts of his family? His concentration lapses could be a sign that his shields were at risk of being breached.

Simon had no financial need to work and presumably could spend his days playing polo and doing whatever else the super-rich did to pass their time, yet he chose to work in a demanding profession. Despite his background, he was at ease around most people, and he had correctly pulled him up on viewing Rob's actions through a middle-class prism.

Peter finished his coffee and carried it along with his plate to the sink. He should be focussing on Rob and Jane, not dissecting Simon. Especially as he still harboured doubts about Rob's innocence.

As they lacked an unbiased opinion of Rob's relationship with Jane, he decided to drive out to Crowcombe to speak to their neighbours, including the one who had overheard them arguing. In addition to commenting on the relationship, one of them might be, or know, the mystery late-night dog walker.

It occurred to him that the journalist who had reported on Chris' eviction might have researched the family's financial situation for his article, and he might know if Jane received an inheritance worth killing for. Not wanting to step on Simon's toes, Peter rang him to see if he had heard back from the reporter. Simon didn't answer, so he left a quick message saying he was driving out to Crowcombe and would catch up with him later.

Surrounded by open countryside, the town of Crowcombe came into view as an unexpected surprise. The town's outskirts were a combination of upmarket, small housing developments with open spaces and local shops. As he drove closer to the centre, the houses became older, mostly built of Cotswold stone with slated tile roofs.

The cars slowed to a crawl on streets not built for the current level of traffic, giving him the chance to take a good look around. There was the usual array of major well-known stores alongside an impressive array of independent stores incorporated into the old buildings. A stone bandstand, a clock tower and a large war memorial added to the charm of the town centre.

As he left the centre, the traffic started to thin and speed up. On this side of town, the residential area comprised older-style houses linked by a warren of narrow lanes, many following a one-way system.

Jane's home was at the end of a narrow no-through road. The closer he came to the house, the narrower the lane became. He pulled into the paved driveway enclosed by a stone wall. Getting out of his car, he wondered if the paved area had once been a front garden. Walking out past the wall and looking back along the lane, he could see every house was distinct from its neighbours, built to individual styles at different times. Although he knew he was less than a mile from the town centre, the lane had the feel of a village community. The well-tended houses and gardens suggested it was a settled community, with residents who had plenty of free time or could afford to pay someone for the upkeep.

As he had called ahead, he already knew the neighbour who overheard the argument between Rob and Jane was in, but the number of parked cars in the driveways suggested so were many others. Peter put it down to a combination of good luck and it being the type of area where young mothers could afford to stay home, and people retired to or never left.

CHAPTER TWENTY-FIVE

Bang on time, Peter rang the bell to Primrose House, Bill Broderick's home, and stood back to wait for the door to be opened. "Hello, it's Peter Hatherall. We spoke on the phone this morning."

"Come in, we've been expecting you," Bill said, leading the way past two golf bags. "Off with the wife to play a round of golf once you've finished with me. This way."

As they entered an open-plan living area, Bill's wife stood up from the sofa, dressed in tailored trousers and a light sweater. "I'll leave you two to it. Would you like something to drink before I go?"

"A coffee would be lovely," Peter said. "Milk, no sugar, but don't feel you must leave on my account. I would value your input if you could rejoin us."

"One for me too, Sandra," Bill said before sitting. "How can I help you? We were interviewed by the police the day it happened. Poor Sandra still has nightmares about it. It's not the type of thing that happens around here, and it gave us all a terrible shock."

"I can imagine," Peter said, settled in a comfortable armchair that smelt brand new. "I understand you heard them arguing the night before."

Bill ran a hand through his thinning hair. "Yes, and I've asked myself a thousand times since why I didn't call the police to report the disturbance. The simple answer is I never thought in my wildest dreams that something so awful could happen right next door to us. Rob was a little rough around the edges, but he seemed a decent enough bloke. We often spoke over the garden fence if we were doing a spot of gardening or car maintenance, and we've been to several of their barbeques. They were always very generous hosts."

"Did you get along with Jane as well?"

"Yes. A lovely lady. She was far classier than Rob, but we were pleased she had found somebody who seemed to care for her. We worried before about her being lonely. We frequently invited her to join us for a game of golf, but she said it wasn't her thing. I think she was quite shy. Rob brought her out of herself, and we always thought they seemed so happy together. I guess it just goes to show that you can never really tell what goes on behind closed doors."

Peter furrowed his forehead as the theory of Rob isolating Jane went out the window. "Had you ever heard them argue loudly before?"

"Once or twice, we've heard raised voices and slammed doors, but nothing like that evening."

"What was different about that evening's row?"

"It was particularly loud and followed by the sound of crashing and things being thrown around. Before, it was the odd raised voice and maybe a slammed door."

"Can you confirm the time you heard the disturbance and whether you're sure it was Rob and Jane you heard?"

"It was ten minutes to eight, and I'm sure it was them."

"That's a very precise time, and why are you so sure?"

"There was a programme we wanted to see on television that was due to start at eight." Pulling a face, Bill said, "Sandra had burnt supper earlier. We were just about to settle down in front of the television when she remembered she had left the kitchen window open to let the smoke out. As I was closing it, I heard a loud crash coming from their house, followed by them shouting at one another and what sounded like things being thrown around. I didn't want to be nosy, so I shut the window and wiped down the kitchen counter. I was about to return to the living room when I saw Rob storm out of the house."

"Were they both shouting?"

Bill paused as he recalled the incident. "It was mostly Jane, but I heard Rob as well."

"Did you see Jane later that evening or hear any other noises?"

They were interrupted by Sandra, bringing in a tray of coffee and biscuits. Offering the tray to Peter, Sandra said, "Help yourself. There's a selection of biscuits to choose from."

When they were resettled, Bill said, "I was just telling Peter how I saw Rob march out of next door that night. We didn't hear any other noises coming from the house afterwards, did we?"

"I certainly didn't. We were watching TV, but I think we would have heard if it had started up again."

"Did you hear the earlier shouting that evening, Sandra?" Peter asked.

"No, but I was in here having a last-minute tidy-up, and the door to the kitchen was closed to keep the smell and the draft from the window out. I always find it's when I'm quietly sitting down that I hear strange noises."

"Do you remember what time you went to bed that night?"

Bill and Sandra looked blankly at each other. "I think we went up straight after the programme finished," Sandra said. "So that would have been shortly after ten."

"I told the police I heard two cars later that evening, but the police didn't seem that interested," Bill said. "Don't ask me what time it was. The first one woke me up, but I was able to go straight back to sleep, so I didn't check the time. I'm not certain, but as I was drifting off, I think there was another vehicle."

"Do you remember where it came from?"

"It was close. There are only four houses at this end of the lane. There's a walkthrough to the next street, but you can't drive a vehicle through there."

"How about you, Sandra? Did you hear anything?"

"No, but then I'm a heavy sleeper. Once I shut my eyes, I'm gone for the night."

"Never mind. It's helpful to know about the vehicles. I can ask your neighbours if they heard anything," Peter said. "One more thing before I go. Do you know anyone who walks a terrier-type dog very late at night? After eleven o'clock?"

"No, I'm afraid I don't. We're early birds and are often in bed by ten o'clock," Bill said. "I'll ask around if that would help."

"That would be brilliant," Peter said. He stood and handed over his card. "If you hear anything about the cars, the dog walker or anything else that might be useful, please call me."

Sandra remained seated, but Bill stood. "Do you think he did it?"

"I don't know," Peter admitted. "Do you?"

"Before it happened, I would have said absolutely not. They seemed a happy, normal couple, but what do we know? We were neighbourly, but not best friends."

CHAPTER TWENTY-SIX

Peter left Bill and Sandra to knock on Jane's other neighbour's door. Receiving no reply, he tried the remaining houses at the top of the lane. There had been no mention of it in the brief statements the police had taken at the time, but one of them having guests that evening would easily explain the two cars and their lack of interest. Only two residents were in, but they both said they hadn't heard anything that night and couldn't remember seeing additional cars parked nearby.

Finally, he crossed the lane to the house opposite Bill and Sandra. A young woman holding a baby answered the door. After he explained who he was, she invited him in. "We'll go into the kitchen if that's okay. My husband is working from home today, and we're trying not to disturb him," she said, wiggling one of the baby's chubby legs.

Not remembering seeing one, Peter asked, "Did the police take a statement from you the following day?"

"No, they knocked on the door, but when I said we had been out at a dinner party that night, they weren't interested in speaking to me. My husband had already left for his usual Saturday cycle ride, so they didn't speak to him at all."

"Did you have a babysitter that night?"

Moving the smiling baby over to her other hip, Judy replied, "No, it was at a friend's house, and as Pearl is such an easy baby, we took her with us."

"Later that night when you returned home, did you see or hear a car on this end of the lane?"

"Sorry. We stayed at our friend's house overnight and drove back first thing in the morning."

"I see," Peter said, disappointed at receiving a blank. He could try the two houses lower down the lane, but from there, it would be hard to distinguish between cars driving on their lane and those travelling along the road at the bottom.

"But I did see Rob the following morning," Judy said. "I happened to be looking out of the living room window when he was walking up his driveway. It would have been around eight o'clock. It's only an impression, but he didn't look like someone who thought anything was wrong. He was just walking casually, carrying a bunch of flowers. I remember thinking, what's he apologising for? After he opened the front door to go in, he bent down to pick up the post and closed the door behind him. Ten minutes or so later, I heard the sirens outside when I was feeding Pearl. I was going to go over to see what had happened, but then I saw Rob being taken away in a police car. The police told me about Jane's death when they knocked on my door. I wouldn't believe it at first. It was so shocking."

"How well did you know Rob and Jane?"

"Just as neighbours. They held a few barbeques and always invited us over."

"Did you go?"

"A couple of times. They were fun, relaxed events. We liked them," Judy said, chewing her lip. "I still can't get my head around it. Rob was always so friendly and attentive to Jane."

"Did you ever hear them arguing or notice any tension between them?"

"We probably bicker more than they did," Judy said. "All I can say is they seemed an ordinary couple to me. Something very dramatic must have happened for him to do what he did."

"Did you see anything of his daughter, Lucy?"

"Not so much, but she was polite and would wave if she saw us."

"Do you think your husband could tell us anything more?"

"He hasn't said anything, and he has Zoom meetings all

morning, so I would prefer not to disturb him right now. Like most men, he's not exactly observant. I can talk to him later, and I'll call you if he does know something."

Peter stood and held over his card. "That would be helpful. I don't suppose you know an older man who walks his dog late at night? It's a terrier or something similar."

"I think I know who you mean. I've seen him, but I don't know who he is, and I haven't seen him recently. He's elderly and usually huddled in a coat and hat, so I can't give you a clear description. I noticed him when Pearl was still having late-night feeds. She sleeps right through now," Judy said, looking proudly at her baby.

Peter spoke to the residents living lower down the lane, but none of them could add anything more than how shocked they were by the murder. He returned to his car and checked his phone. He had turned it to silent while speaking to the neighbours, and he expected to see a return call from Simon. There were no messages or missed calls, and when he called Simon's number, there was no answer.

The comments he'd heard about Rob from his neighbours, left him feeling stumped. It was rare for no one to have a bad word to say about someone arrested for suspected murder. Usually, at least one person said they had always had doubts. His friends and his daughter standing by him were one thing, but these were people who barely knew him. The opinion that he brought Jane out of her shell also had been repeated. So much for him being a controlling partner. The only person bad-mouthing him was Chris.

After a moment of indecision, Peter called the journalist. He replied straight away and said he had been trying to return Simon's call. As he lived only fifteen miles away in Sturminster, they arranged to meet in a farm café nearby that the journalist recommended.

CHAPTER TWENTY-SEVEN

As soon as Peter walked into the bustling cafe, the reporter introduced himself as Eddie and ordered a coffee for Peter and a fresh cup of tea for himself. "I'll come clean from the start and admit that due to a past grudge, I enjoyed every minute of reporting on the great Chris Forbes being evicted. It couldn't have happened to a nicer bloke."

"Why the grudge?" Peter asked, sipping his coffee.

"We grew up in the same village. Well, he was up at the big house, I was down in the village," Eddie said. "He went to a fancy school but was at home at weekends and during the holidays. If I said he was an arrogant bully, that wouldn't adequately cover it. He was vile. My little sister still has a scar on her face to show for it."

"Oh? What happened?"

"She was sitting on our garden wall minding her own business, when he rode by on his horse and struck her across the face with his riding crop for no reason. She came running into the house with blood pouring down her face."

"For no reason at all?"

"His beef was with me," Eddie said. "I had called him out the week before for pushing younger kids around, and the parents had words about it. A few days later, my mum's car was keyed. It wasn't hard to work out who by. He was bad enough as a kid, but he was even worse as an adult. He drove his car at ridiculous speeds. How he didn't kill someone is beyond me. Every once in a while, he would turn up at village events or the pub, generally drunk and always boorish and rude. Nobody could stand him, but because of his family's standing in the area, few tackled him about his behaviour. He was especially unpleasant to the local girls, either groping them or calling them ugly. He believed he was someone untouchable, so you can imagine how ecstatic we all were about his eviction."

"Did he have any friends in the village?"

"Not one."

"How about his sister?"

"She was just plain odd. She was rarely seen outside of the house, and when she was, she wore odd clothes. Outfits with frilly collars and long sleeves that looked like they belonged in the last century."

"But she didn't throw her weight around in the same way as her brother?"

Eddie shook his head. "I'm not sure I ever heard her speak. Most people assumed there was something wrong with her. She never used to look anything like the picture posted in the newspaper after she was murdered. I didn't recognise her. When I saw the name, I double-checked it was her."

"Do you still live in the village?"

"I couldn't afford it," Eddie said. "No, I moved into a flat in Birstall when I got my first job. I was working for the Birstall Post when I heard about that pompous twit's financial problems and begged for the chance to report on it. My parents were still alive and living in the village then. They said very little had changed. Chris was still an arrogant loudmouth, and his sister took care of their parents, who were getting on by then."

"Do you know how Chris lost his money?"

"Everyone knows how he lost his money," Eddie said. "A combination of betting big money on the horses and throwing money around on a champagne lifestyle he couldn't afford. Without the gambling and a bit of prudent investing, he probably could have continued his lifestyle without doing a day's work, but I was over the moon to see his downfall."

"Do you know who he owed money to?"

"A shorter list would be people he didn't owe money to," Eddie said. "He was moving in flashy circles, throwing large sums of money around like confetti. They dropped him like a stone when he couldn't keep up. Rumour had it that when the banks started saying no, he went to more dubious lenders. The sort that applies high interest rates and even stricter penalties for payment defaults. After listening to your colleague's message, I looked back over my notes and jotted down a couple of names." Eddie bent down to the bag at his feet and pulled out a sheet of paper. "These are some of the people I believe he *may* have owed money to. I wanted to delve deeper at the time, but the newspaper wouldn't fund an investigation. I was ambitious to get on back then and had plenty of other assignments, so I let it go."

Peter took the typed sheet. He didn't recognise any of the names, but they were worth following up on. "Thanks," he said, folding the paper and slipping it into his pocket. "You're the second person who has mentioned Jane transformed herself after her parents' death. Do you know anyone who might have been in contact with her during that time?"

"Sorry. She's not someone I've ever taken an interest in. She was that type of person."

"What sort of money would she have inherited from her parents?"

"They were comfortably off, but after death duties and all that, I wouldn't know."

After Eddie left, Peter rang Simon again. This time, he answered, although he sounded groggy. He told Peter he was following up on a lead on someone Chris owed money to. Peter read out the names that Eddie had given him, and they agreed to meet back at the office that evening.

CHAPTER TWENTY-EIGHT

Simon opened one eye when Albert started to bark at the bedroom door to go out. Putting a pillow over his head failed to block out the noise or soothe his pounding headache. Accepting the pain wouldn't stop until he let the dogs out, he slowly hauled himself out of bed. He pulled on his dressing gown and opened the door. Both dogs shot past him and ran down the stairs. Holding the bannisters, Simon gingerly followed. He opened the back door and left it ajar for the dogs to come back in once they were done. Bleary-eyed, he set up the coffee machine and reached for his mobile phone. He groaned when he saw the battery was flat and plugged it in to recharge.

Simon slumped at the kitchen table with his head resting on his outstretched arms. He really shouldn't have had that last drink. When would he finally learn to know his limit? Learn to get to the point where his darkness receded, but to go no further.

He raised his head when the dogs bounded back into the room, full of energy. They nudged his legs, wondering when their walk would start, or failing that, when their breakfast would arrive. "Okay, boys. I need a coffee first, and then we'll see if a walk will clear my head."

Simon dragged himself across the room to collect his coffee and his phone still attached to the charger. His first sip of coffee made him feel a little better, and his phone had enough power for him to check his messages. There were messages and unanswered calls from Peter, Kate and the journalist. Dick had promised to call him back with more details about the man he heard Chris owed large sums of money to, but he hadn't called.

A plan of sorts formed in Simon's mind. After he had walked and fed the dogs, he would call Kate to say he had walked the dogs through Hinnegar Woods, where phone reception was patchy. Then, he would chase Dick for more precise details and call Peter to say he was spending the day following up on an important lead concerning Chris' financial situation. He would call the journalist later and arrange to see him tomorrow.

He glanced at the sink full of dirty plates and the empty bottles of wine on the counter. He could leave it for now, but he should probably try to tidy up before Kate returned.

If only he could clear the mess in his head so easily. His tangled emotions were why he hadn't asked Kate to marry him. He worked hard to disguise it, but the anger and confusion never went away. He couldn't offer her stability when sometimes he felt he was hanging on by the thinnest of threads. His darkness threatening to consume him was an ever-present threat, and he was tired of fighting it. He loved her, but he could never marry her without his family being there. Their absence would be unbearable. The bottom line was he didn't deserve her, so he would have to let her go.

An hour later, the dogs woke Simon by pawing his leg. Seeing the time, he jumped up, grabbed the dog leads from the back of the door and set off for a quick walk around the three fields behind the house. He made a deal with the dogs that if they didn't tell, he would give them an extra big breakfast when they returned.

After the walk, Simon started to feel more human. While tidying away the wine bottles and clothes he had left lying around the kitchen, he rang Dick. Gladys answered and said Dick couldn't come to the phone due to a family bereavement and abruptly hung up. Staring at the phone, Simon tried to remember the scant details Dick had given about his family.

Simon called Dick's number, and Gladys answered again. "I told you. Dick is indisposed."

"Can you pass on my condolences?"

"Will do," Gladys said before the phone went dead again.

Simon sighed and replayed the garbled message that Dick had left on his phone about the man Chris was heavily involved with. From the stereotypical description, Simon suspected Daryl Jee was a figment of Dick's imagination and decided to leave contacting him until he had spoken to Dick again.

In his message, Dick said Daryl was Irish, walked with a limp and was an ex-jockey who had been barred from the Jockey Club for something or other. He made a living selling inside racing stories and tips and providing guaranteed winners at a price, with a sideline in money lending and laundering. He was rumoured to be engaged in race fixing and various other dodgy activities surrounding the world of gambling. His regular haunt was Sam Johnson Bookmakers. Simon would easily recognise him as he was short, lacked his two front teeth and had looks only a mother could appreciate.

Simon was about to call the journalist instead when Peter rang. Despite his reservations before meeting him, he liked Peter and wanted to impress him, so he told a story of how he had discovered Chris had a history with Daryl and was close to tracking the ex-jockey down. Peter seemed to believe the story and gave him a list of other names to check out alongside Daryl.

CHAPTER TWENTY-NINE

After a quick shower, feeling he had no other option, Simon punched the address for Sam Johnson Bookmakers into his car's navigation system and set off in search of a figment of Dick's imagination. A fool's errand if ever he had heard one, but he needed something to show for the day when he met Peter later.

He arrived without incident and parked a few doors down from the bookies. Most other businesses on the narrow side street were boarded up with steel metal gates. The only ones still operating were a small Irish pub and a fish and chips shop. A group of men smoking roll-ups in an empty doorway gave him a cursory glance as he walked through the bookie's entrance.

Simon sat on an uncomfortable stool bolted to the floor facing a narrow ledge. Above it was a row of televisions, showing different horse races and betting odds. The row of televisions behind him showed football and cricket matches. To his left, an older man muttered to himself while watching the screens. Behind him, a man and a woman sat separately with their eyes glued to the screen. Another man stood near the window overlooking the street. A bored-looking younger man watched him from inside a booth protected by a glass screen.

The isolation of the people sharing their interests and body odours added to Simon's low mood. The only positive was that they were so locked in their own misery that they were oblivious to anything happening around them, so he could stop worrying about looking conspicuous. He fitted in perfectly.

On the ledge in front of Simon was a pen attached by a chain and a pile of fresh betting slips. Feeling out of his depth, he focussed on one screen and blocked out the sound from the others, trying to follow what was going on so he could place a bet. He had placed bets before at the racetrack. Those outings had involved champagne and dressing up, but they had given him a rough understanding of form and odds. The weight of his privileged background bore down on him in the alien environment as he tried to fill out the betting slips.

Before his life had been thrown upside down, he had had no concept of how lucky he was or what an arrogant, spoilt idiot he was. Mixed up with the grief and shock of losing his family, he had grown to resent the pampered lifestyle they had given him, which further fed the self-hatred he hid from everyone. Today was another reminder of how much he had been sheltered from everyday life.

When he completed his slip, he found the race was about to start, so he was too late. He screwed up the slip and looked at the form of the horses due to run in the next race. A group of giggling girls came in and started filling out slips to his right. They had been drinking and found everything hysterically funny. He waited a while and then followed them up to the booth with his completed slip.

When he reached the counter, the young man gave him a sympathetic smile and asked, "First time? Do you need any help?"

Simon handed over his slip and money, and replied, "My first time in here." When given the computerised receipt, he said, "I was told Daryl might be here today."

A muscle twitched in the man's jaw, although his expression remained blank. "I don't know anyone by that name."

"Oh? I heard he came in here regularly. An ex-jockey missing his front teeth?"

"Nah. I can't help you. That description doesn't ring any bells. Good luck with the race."

As Simon returned to his stool to watch the race, the older man caught his eye and beckoned him over. He pulled Simon closer and asked, "What you got? Has Daryl given you a name for the big race?"

"Sorry, no," Simon said. "I heard he might be here today. Do you know him?"

"Of him," the man said, releasing his hold on Simon and reverting to muttering as he stared at the screens.

Simon tried to make himself comfortable on his stool and studied the horses running in the following race. While he waited for the race to start, a man entered and walked straight to the booth to place a bet before sitting by himself in the corner. It occurred to Simon that people came here for peace and quiet, and he silently mocked his limited understanding of life. What did he know about anything?

He looked up at the screen as the race started. The horses' bulging muscles and the excitement in the air were palpable. He was distracted by a woman walking in to speak to the man in the corner and leaving again. He strained to hear what was said but couldn't hear anything over the race commentator's high-pitched, excited voice.

The horses were closely bunched together as they entered the final stages, and it looked like any of them could win. In the blur, he couldn't see his horse's colours. Two horses broke from the pack and galloped neck and neck to the finishing line. As the commentator announced it was a photo finish, Simon looked for where his horse had finished. It hadn't. It had unseated its rider in the earlier stages when he had been distracted.

Simon looked down at the pile of betting slips. He had experienced the thrill of the race for a moment, but did he want to waste all afternoon waiting for someone who probably wouldn't come in? It wasn't as though he could start a chance conversation with anyone, and with the race finished, the air of depression had returned.

Glancing out the window, he could see the pub across the road had opened. A few tables and chairs had been set up on the pavement outside, although the group of men smoking had disappeared. He could just as easily sit there in the weak sunshine and watch the entrance for another half hour before giving up on seeing Daryl. Customers in the pub would be more likely to speak to him, and a few drinks would relax him. He nodded a farewell to the man in the booth, who looked away, avoiding eye contact.

CHAPTER THIRTY

Simon hesitated in the doorway, swallowing his fear. If he went back inside, it would only delay the inevitable. The street was deserted other than a man with tattooed knuckles casually sitting on the bonnet of his car. He looked along the empty street. In his mind's eye, all it lacked was tumbleweed and someone out of sight whistling a haunting tune.

There was no point pretending it wasn't his car and bolting. Chances are there was someone else waiting in case he did just that. He kicked himself for leaving the car registered to his address outside. He should have parked a couple of streets away and walked. He curled his hand around his phone in his pocket and strolled over to the car, looking down until he was directly in front of the stranger. Praying it wouldn't come out as a squeak, he said, "Hi. Can I help you?"

A flat cap partially covered the man's weather-beaten face, but the colour of his drooping jowls and broken nose suggested he was a heart attack waiting to happen. His sturdy boots and worn wax jacket might indicate he spent time outdoors in the fresh air, but he wasn't following a healthy diet and lifestyle. Simon couldn't see the man's eyes under the hat, but he imagined they bulged under the strain of high blood pressure.

"I doubt it," the stranger said in a heavy Northern Irish accent. "Have any luck?"

"No. Unseated the rider." Simon's mouth dried as the man placed one of his pudgy hands in his jacket pocket.

"Heard you were looking for Daryl."

"Well, umm. Not really," Simon stuttered. "Someone told me he always had good tips. I might have had more luck if he had been around. But anyway, nice to meet you. I had best be on my way."

"Not so fast. Who told you to come looking for Daryl here?"

"I've placed my bet and lost, so it doesn't matter now."

"It does to me. Who are you?"

"Me? I'm just a nobody who fancied a flutter," Simon replied.

"You probably are, but who sent you?"

"Sent me? No one."

The man pulled a knife from his pocket and used it to clean his fingernails. "Who said Daryl was going to be here?"

"I can't remember," Simon said, as his mind went blank on any possible random combination of names. "Umm … Mike Bell."

"Never heard of him. Do you want to meet Daryl or not."

"Like I said, not anymore, no."

"Fair enough. But try again with the name of the person who sent you."

Simon squirmed as he watched the continuing manicure. "Well, if I'm perfectly honest, nobody sent me. I happened to overhear a conversation in a pub."

"People don't take that much notice of random overheard opinions." Moving the knife from hand to hand, the man tilted his head to look at Simon. "I never forget a face. I'm just asking nicely for a name. Daryl likes to know who is talking about him."

"It was a throwaway comment I overheard. This guy was just saying he was someone who came here and always had good tips."

"Then you won't mind giving me his name. If that was all it was, then no one has anything to worry about. If it was someone badmouthing him, then that would be a different matter."

"Oh, he wasn't doing that."

"Look, kid. I can see you're nobody of note, but I need a name from you. If it's as innocent as you say, then that'll be an end to it. But I am getting very tired of talking to you and would hate to have to take things further."

"Okay, I'll tell you, but I swear it was an innocent comment I overheard. The guy was saying how good his tips were," Simon said, stalling for time. He doubted Dick's name would be any more memorable to the guy than the made-up name, plus he didn't want to hand over a friend's name. He couldn't imagine that these people would consider Chris a threat, but as a serious gambler, his name might be known. It would tie in with his story that he hoped to receive a good tip. "Okay. I don't know him, but I believe the guy I overheard was Chris Forbes."

"Thank you. That was easy, wasn't it." The man slipped the knife back into his pocket. "You get on your way, lad. And I've got a tip for you. Stay away from the horses."

"Thank you," Simon said, walking around the man to get into his car.

CHAPTER THIRTY-ONE

With shaking hands, Simon turned his car towards home. His head was bombarded with violent scenarios of what might have happened, and he had no appetite for contacting any of the men on Peter's list if they were of the same ilk as Daryl. Whoever that guy on his car was, he wasn't someone you wanted to cross, and Simon hoped he would never bump into him again. He wondered how on earth Dick had heard about Daryl. Dick wasn't the most upstanding of citizens, but he didn't mix in those sorts of circles.

Even in the privacy of his car, his face flushed. He accepted he was a coward but why was he such an idiot as well? Once he had been smart. School teachers said he was intelligent, but now his brain didn't work properly, and he lurched from one bad decision to another.

He couldn't imagine Peter, or anyone else, approaching the matter the way he had. And for what? His stupid pride. He didn't want Peter to think he was an incompetent fool. And how did he set out to do that? By being an incompetent fool. He needed to sort out his head and start to think straight.

By the time he stopped shaking, he had pulled one positive from the experience. For a long time, he had thought he wanted to die and had considered the different ways he could achieve his aim. He had convinced himself that only Kate's arrival was delaying things. Watching the thug with the knife, he realised that he wasn't ready to die. He had put himself in dangerous situations before, thinking he didn't care whether he survived, but today's encounter had shaken him to the core. In a roundabout way he had made some progress. All he had to do was work out how to resolve the rest of the mess buzzing around his brain.

As his fears subsided, he started to feel the effects of his drinking the night before. And he was hungry. The way his day was going, it would be safer to call it a day. He could hit the ground running tomorrow to make up for it. If he was planning to stick around long-term, he needed to get a grip on a lot of things and to do that, he needed food, a good sleep and a clear head.

The dogs were pleased to see him home. To make up for their earlier short walk, Simon picked up their leads and set off with them across the fields to the woods to clear his head. It was a complete coincidence that the area lacked phone reception.

When he returned with tired, happy dogs, he made himself a coffee and called Dick's mobile, hoping Gladys wouldn't answer again.

"Ah, Simon. My good fellow," Dick boomed. "You've returned my calls at last."

"I wasn't aware you had called," Simon said. His phone blipped, notifying him of a series of missed calls. "The notification has just come through. I can't have had a clear signal earlier."

"Where are you?"

"At home," Simon said suspiciously. He was starting his new life tomorrow, and he didn't want to let Peter down again. One drink with Dick always led to several more.

"Excellent. I've contacted you in time," Dick said. "That name I gave you before. It was a mistake."

"You mean Daryl?"

"Shh. I've never heard or mentioned that name before."

"But you did," Simon said.

"Under intense torture, I would deny everything. Don't go anywhere near him."

"I wish you had told me that last night," Simon muttered. "Why was it a mistake?"

"If Chris Forbes owes him money, he's insane. Is he insane?" Before Simon could reply, Dick continued, "I can't imagine he's involved with him anyway, and he's not someone you want to meet. Not that I know who you are talking about."

"Why the changed story?"

"Sorry, I'm not talking about it anymore, and that's final."

"Okay, fine," Simon said. His head was pounding, he felt nauseous and forgetting about the whole thing was a good idea. "Did Gladys pass on my condolences yesterday? She said you've lost someone."

"Yes, my dear, darling Colin."

"That lovely, little dog of yours? I'm so sorry. She was lovely."

Dick swallowed a sob. "Thank you so much for your kind words. It's good to have someone to talk about her to. Gladys doesn't understand the ache in my heart. She can be so hard sometimes. She's even talking about puppies."

"That's far too soon," Simon said. "These things take time."

"I knew you would understand when no one else does. My grief is real. It feels like my heart is breaking." After a bout of sobbing, Dick said, "I don't suppose you want to come over? Colin deserves a wake, and you're the only one who understands."

Simon felt his resolve slip. He looked down at Alfred and Albert and imagined how he would feel when their time came. "Is Gladys really not helping you through this?"

"Not at all. She's sulking about having to cancel dancing. How could she be so cruel? I don't think I'll ever be able to dance again. I feel so empty," Dick wailed.

"Okay. Give me an hour, and I'll be over with a couple of bottles," Simon said, hoping his liver would survive one final pounding before he called a day on drinking. There was no point saying he wouldn't drink to excess with Dick as it would be a lie.

Brightening, Dick asked, "Should Gladys make up the spare room?"

"Kate's away, so I'll have to get home at some point. I'll book a taxi."

Simon wandered around the kitchen and opened and closed

cupboard doors, looking for something simple to make for supper. It had to be something substantial to soak up the alcohol he was going to drink. Gladys would probably feed him snacks throughout the evening unless it was a severe sulk, but he couldn't rely on her unpredictable nature. He popped a couple of pieces of bread in the toaster to keep his strength up while he searched. He was biting into it when his phone rang.

"Ah, Peter. Sorry. I was about to ring you."

"I thought you were popping into the office?"

"I was, only something has come up. A good friend has rung in a bad way. I'm grabbing something to eat and heading out to be with him. He's not usually so melodramatic," Simon lied. "I feel I need to check he's okay."

"Fair enough. We can make an early start tomorrow. Say, eight-thirty, meet in the office?"

"How about mid-morning? I have a couple of things to follow up on."

"Okay. How did your lead work out?"

"A dead end." Simon launched into an explanation of what had happened at the bookies, although he was nonchalant about the conversation outside. In his version, he had kept control of the situation.

"You parked your car directly outside? You know they could use your car's registration number to track you down? They only need to claim it was in a minor accident."

"They weren't interested in me," Simon said, more to convince himself than Peter. "They only wanted to know how I knew about Daryl."

"What name did you give them?"

"A false one didn't work, so I said Chris Forbes. I claimed I overheard him say positive things about Daryl in a pub, so there won't be any comeback."

"Let's hope you're right," Peter said. "I hope your friend is okay, and I'll see you mid-morning tomorrow."

CHAPTER THIRTY-TWO

Peter woke up in a bad mood. After making the effort to go up to bed the previous evening, he was disturbed by a telephone call in the early hours. It was all the more frustrating because he couldn't act on it until the police had completed their initial enquiries. It wasn't the young constable's fault, it had been good of him to call, but he had to thank him through gritted teeth. Riled up by the news, he'd been unable to get back to sleep.

He stopped only for a coffee before heading towards Simon's home. His resolve to be more understanding of Simon after hearing about his past was weakened by his lack of sleep, and he was sure he wouldn't catch him following up on leads, as he claimed. Everyone has problems, and last night's news superseded the agreement for him to have a lie in.

Simon was woken by his dogs barking and jumping up at the bedroom window. He threw a pillow at them to stop, and it took a while for him to realise the pounding was coming from downstairs, not from inside his head. Groggy and unsteady on his feet, he pulled on his dressing gown and carefully negotiated the stairs. "Okay. I'm coming." He opened the front door to Peter who was looking as fresh as a daisy. "What time is it?"

"You look dreadful. Do you want me to put some coffee on while you get dressed?"

Simon stood in a confused state as his dogs shot out the door. "Umm. Come in. Leave the door open for the dogs," he said, leading the way to the kitchen. Setting up the coffee machine, he asked, "Has something happened? I thought we weren't meeting until later."

"You could say that," Peter said sharply. Simon obviously had a skinful the night before, and his patience with him was wearing thin. "Chris Forbes was beaten up last night. He's in hospital, and I've been told it's not looking good," Peter said, watching the little colour it had, drain from Simon's face.

"Do you think it was related to my visit yesterday?"

"That's what we're going to find out."

"I'll go and get dressed."

When Simon returned to the kitchen, Peter shoved a mug of coffee in his hand. "Are you sure you're up to this?" Simon had splashed some water on his face while getting dressed, but he still looked awful.

"I'll be fine once I've drunk this," Simon said, raising his mug. "Once I've fed the dogs, I'll be good to go. Where are we going?"

"Straight to the hospital. We might not be able to speak to Chris, but it's worth a go. I can't imagine there's a line of visitors waiting to see him. I told the officers who found him about his sister and your botched visit to the bookies yesterday, but they weren't overly interested. They were viewing it as one more drunk getting into a fight."

"It wasn't botched," Simon started to object.

Peter shot Simon a stern look to silence him. "We'll then visit DI Ford, the officer handling Jane's murder investigation. You need to tell him exactly what happened outside the bookies. And you need to tell me who tipped you off about Daryl."

"I don't think that will be necessary," Simon said. "I spoke to my contact last night, and I doubt there is any connection to my visit. If there is, then it was accidental."

"What do you mean accidental?" Peter asked, failing to keep his rising irritation from his tone.

"Umm … my source doesn't know Daryl or even whether he knew Chris. It was just a name he had heard of, so questioning him further won't achieve anything," Simon said. "It was a lucky guess, or an unlucky one, depending on how you want to view it."

"It's too much of a coincidence to let it go," Peter said. "I need to know why your contact gave you that name. He must have had a reason."

"Not necessarily," Simon mumbled.

"His name?"

"He's just a guy I know from the pub. He won't know anything."

"Called?"

"Dick Death."

"As in Dick and Gladys?" Peter said, running a hand through his hair in frustration. "I thought you had a proper contact who actually knew something about the gambling world. I'm not sure Dick knows how to put his underpants on the right way around. God help me. Your contact was Dick!"

Simon remained silent in the car, staring glumly out the window, saying nothing while Peter reeled his temper back in. He may have expected too much of Simon and should have taken more notice when Charlie said he needed to be supervised. The silence grew uncomfortable, and Peter groaned at the thought of spending the rest of the day dancing around Simon's childish sulk. He forced an even tone and asked, "Was Dick also your friend in need last night?"

Simon sheepishly mumbled, "Yes."

Peter could see Simon looking paler by the minute, and he regretted dragging him along as a petty form of punishment. He should have left him to sleep off his hangover. "You're not going to be sick, are you?"

"I'm fine, just thinking," Simon replied. He didn't speak again until Peter drove into the hospital car park. "I've had a thought. What if everyone has it all wrong, and the attack on Chris is directly related to his sister's murder, but it has nothing to do with my visit? Is it possible Chris and Jane were up to something together and stepped on the wrong toes? They didn't get what they wanted from Jane, so they came back for Chris."

"How convenient, as that also solves your guilty conscience," Peter couldn't stop himself from snapping. Having a go at Simon wasn't going to help the situation. He sighed and added in a softer voice, "It's possible."

"We know the trust fund didn't exist, but they were meeting up, and money was changing hands."

"I spoke to Lucy again, and she says that Chris only pestered Jane about once every month, and the conversations were always brief. That doesn't seem long enough if they had some sort of ongoing business."

"As far as Lucy knows," Simon says. "Who's to say they weren't in regular contact without her or Rob knowing? We don't know Jane wasn't meeting her brother on work breaks or whenever she said she was popping to the shops."

"I won't dismiss the idea entirely, but I think you are clutching at straws. There's been nothing to suggest any clandestine meetings, and Jane's telephone records were thoroughly checked. The only person she called regularly was Rob," Peter said, pulling into a parking place.

"Okay. Going back to something you mentioned before," Simon said. "What if Chris and Rob were the ones with something going on, and Jane was simply in the wrong place at the wrong time."

"Do you have a shred of evidence suggesting that's a possibility?" Peter said, climbing out of the car. "I thought not. Rather than speculating, let's see if Chris will be any more forthcoming today."

Simon followed after him, saying, "At least we won't have one eye on his dogs and the other on his shotgun in here."

Walking on, Peter wasn't sure if Simon was making a dig about his unease around dogs. It wasn't as though he didn't like dogs; he did. Well, some, anyway. But his lifestyle had never allowed for one, and as a constable, he had been called out to a fair few dog attacks. Seeing the damage that they could do, and watching many of them aggressively hurling themselves against makeshift barriers had made him wary.

CHAPTER THIRTY-THREE

Peter asked a disinterested girl behind the hospital reception desk about Chris. Without acknowledging them, she started to tap away on her keyboard. "What's your connection to the patient?"

When Simon leaned across and claimed to be his brother, the receptionist gave him a hard stare. It was unclear whether she believed him, but she gave them directions to his ward.

Striding along the corridor, Peter asked, "Why did you say he was your brother?"

"You're not a police officer anymore, and it's the only way we're going to be allowed to see him if he's that badly hurt."

"She's probably checking your story now, and we'll be turned around at the ward."

"With that queue of people behind us? I doubt it," Simon said confidently.

When they arrived at the ward, Simon used his easy charm and again claimed Chris was his brother. The nurse accepted it without checking and led them to a private side room. Inside, she checked the chart at the foot of the bed before leaving, asking them to keep their visit to under ten minutes.

Chris was conscious but appeared dazed and disorientated. His face was heavily swollen and bruised, and his eyes were little more than slits, but the way he gripped the bed sheets suggested he was terrified by them approaching.

Simon remained standing while Peter pulled a chair up to the side of the bed. "Do you remember us?"

Chris slowly looked between the two of them before giving a slight nod of his head.

"Can you tell us what happened last night?" Peter asked.

Chris shook his head and looked away.

"Was it connected to your sister's death?"

Chris started to try to say something, then pointed to the water bottle with a straw on the other side of his bed. Simon handed it to him, and Chris took a few sips before handing it back. "Leave me alone," he quietly croaked through his split lip.

"We could help you if you tell us who did this," Peter said.

Chris beckoned Simon over. Struggling to get the words out, he said, "Write this down." He went on to give a name and a telephone number. "Ring Ted and ask him to see to the dogs and ponies."

Disappointed it wasn't relevant to their investigation, Simon slipped the note into his pocket but nodded his agreement. "Does he have a key to get in?"

Chris croaked, "He knows where it is," before lying back on his pillows, exhausted from his exertion.

"Now your animals are sorted, can we talk about what happened last night?" Peter asked.

Chris shook his head, mumbled what sounded like no and closed his eyes. After it became clear that Chris wasn't going to say anything more and was possibly asleep, Peter stood and pushed the chair back to where he found it. "Concentrate on getting better. We'll come back in a few days to see you."

CHAPTER THIRTY-FOUR

Crowcombe Police Station was a modern, purpose-built building on the edge of the town. Peter had called ahead, and they were buzzed straight through to meet DI Andrew Ford. He was chatty and friendly as he led them through a plush conference room, insisting they called him Andy.

"They've spent some money on the place," Peter said as he sat.

"It would have been better spent on more officers and support staff, but it is what it is," Andy said. "You said on the phone you had some new information for me."

"Were you passed details of the assault on Chris Forbes last night?"

"No," Andy replied, looking surprised and annoyed.

"I assumed the officers contacted you. I specifically said I thought it likely that it was connected to his sister's murder, and he should be interviewed," Peter said, trying to hide his irritation. He had felt at the time that he wasn't being taken seriously, but he had expected the message to be passed on. As a DCI, he was used to junior officers showing him respect and following up on his suggestions, and he wasn't happy about being ignored. It was a small comfort that Andy looked equally angry at the failure in communication.

"What happened, and how come you heard about it before me?"

Ignoring the second question, Peter said, "It's unclear. I understand the landlord of the Black Horse found him behind the smoking hut when he was locking up for the night."

"Did the landlord recognise him as a customer?" Andy asked.

Peter shook his head. "His own mother wouldn't have recognised him in the state he was in."

Andy sighed. "That pub is as rough as they come. It isn't the sort of place a stranger would wander into unnoticed. If they did, they would soon realise they weren't welcome and walk back out."

"We haven't visited the scene," Peter said. "Is it possible that he wasn't in the pub, as he was found in their rear garden?"

"Access to the pub garden, if you can call a patch of gravel and a tatty smoking hut that, is through the pub, but the fence panels at the back are often broken. I'll make sure there's a full report on my desk by lunchtime."

"Will you be connecting the attack to his sister's murder investigation?"

"That pub is trouble. I'll go through the motions, but I can tell you now that no one in there would have heard or seen anything."

"So, you won't be connecting it to his sister's murder?"

"I didn't say that," Andy said. "Why do you think there's a connection?"

"My colleague here," indicating Simon, "had a run-in with a friend of Daryl Jee's when he was asking some questions about Chris."

"Daryl Jee?"

Peter sensed that Andy had recognised the name and invited Simon to explain his visit to the betting shop. When Simon finished, Peter said, "I don't know if any of this is relevant, but as you're handling the murder investigation, we thought you should know. We are working for Rob's family, but we want to work with you to get to the truth. It does seem strange that Jane's brother has been severely beaten so soon after her death."

Andy raised his eyebrows. "And this happened while we have Mr Lewis in custody, conveniently ruling out his involvement."

"It does suggest there may be an alternative explanation for Jane's murder that needs investigating," Peter said. "You were very quick to home in on Rob as your sole suspect. Was that decision based on something more than the circumstantial evidence and her brother's accusations?"

"Have you read our report?"

"Yes, and everything is circumstantial. I haven't seen one thing that proves Rob's guilt beyond doubt."

"Which is why we're holding him on remand while we complete our enquiries," Andy said wearily. He started to count on his fingers, "He was heard violently arguing with Jane hours before she was killed, he has no alibi other than being drunk on a bench, and there is no other explanation for her death."

"His neighbour said he heard two cars later that night," Peter said. "Has that been followed up on?"

Andy pinched his nose and grimaced. "Until a few months ago that was a through road, and people still try to cut through there, not realising it has been blocked at the top. We would have been more interested if he had heard only one car. Chances are what he heard was a car reaching the top, only to realise it was blocked and turning around to go back."

"But now her brother, who she has financial dealings with, has been severely beaten."

"In a pub renowned for trouble and he also is Rob's accuser," Andy pointed out.

"Does that mean you're not going to expand your investigation?"

"I will look into it," Andy said, flicking his notepad shut. "But we have other reasons to suspect Rob."

"Other than her brother's accusations?"

"Among other things." Andy shrugged and stood. "Thank you for taking the time to come in and pass on this new information."

"Such as?" Peter said. He stood and stepped to the side, blocking Andy's easy path to the door. He expected Andy to refer to the death of Rob's first wife, but there was a slim chance he would mention something else.

"The assault and your story about Daryl," Andy said with a

feigned look of confusion.

"You know that's not what I meant," Peter said. "What other reason do you have for suspecting our client, Rob Lewis? I've read the report and couldn't find anything conclusive. Have you been given access to Jane's final will? Are there other lines of inquiry you haven't shared with us?"

"Do you know about Rob's first wife?"

"We do, and that he was cleared of being involved," Peter said.

"We may be reopening the case."

"Anything else that's not in the official report?"

Andy looked conflicted as he glanced up at the ceiling. He looked Peter directly in the eye, and said, "Sorry, but I can't share the reasons behind a senior officer's operational decisions with you."

"Operational decisions?" Peter queried, before standing to one side to let Andy pass. "Do you agree with them?"

"I will update the DCI on last night's attack, and he will have the final say on how we follow it up. He should be back in the station tomorrow if you want to speak directly to him." Andy briefly smiled before escorting Peter and Simon to the station entrance, where they shook hands.

As soon as they were alone, Simon asked, "What was that about? Operational decisions?"

"I'm not sure, but I think he was hinting at something personal between Rob and his DCI."

"I'm none the wiser," Simon said.

"I need to get you back to your car. After you've arranged the doggy homecare for Chris, I want you to visit Rob again. Put him under as much pressure as possible to see how he reacts, especially what he knew about Jane's will and why he's instructed solicitors over it. Press him on everything he knows about Chris and why he did nothing to stop his meetings with Jane. Also, ask him if he knows Daryl. Once you've done that, contact the other people I gave you yesterday and try to find out how much money Chris currently owes." Peter hit his forehead in frustration. "I forgot to ask about the road camera footage

I requested. It still hasn't turned up. Can you chase it up and ask them to confirm they are sending everything covering the possible routes Chris could have taken that night?"

"Okay," Simon said. "What are you going to be doing?"

"Trying to find out if the DCI has a personal grudge against Rob."

"Would that give us grounds to press for Rob's release?"

Peter shrugged. "We'll be halfway to pushing them to ask wider questions about Jane's death."

"And release Rob?"

"Maybe," Peter said.

CHAPTER THIRTY-FIVE

After dropping Simon off by his car, Peter spent his drive home convincing himself he wasn't heading off on a wild goose chase because of a personal grudge.

After meeting Andy Ford, he was convinced that the DI didn't agree with the way Jane's murder was being handled. He could be reading too much into the exchange, but he thought his lack of enthusiasm for the case stemmed from it being controlled by above.

He had never liked DCI Jack Harris and had been pleased when he left Birkbury station. He was a sexist bully and hated to be crossed. He wouldn't go so far as to say Harris was bent, but he would have no qualms about telling his DI to reach a certain conclusion for personal reasons and ensure he did. Andy didn't strike him as a sloppy officer. If he had been told the only possible outcome was Rob's guilt, it would explain the lack of investigation.

There was no logical explanation for the constable contacting him about the assault on Chris, but not Andy. Before he became too carried away, he would try to discover if the constable's message had been intercepted before reaching him. The annoyed expression on Andy's face suggested the thought had also crossed his mind.

Telling himself his idea wasn't crazy, Peter made himself a coffee and checked through his phone records for the constable's number. His call was answered straight away, and the constable confirmed he had called Crowcombe police station before calling him. He couldn't remember who he spoke to, but he was told his message would be passed to the detectives handling the case as soon as possible.

Peter ended the call and planned where to start his search for his old address book. He remembered it as tatty and falling apart but religiously updated before he finally accepted the digital age and abandoned it. He would start with the boxes in his study, but he expected the search to end up in his attic. He had to work hard to silence the nagging voice insisting his idea was a wacky longshot, even by Simon's standards.

While he drank his coffee, he checked online, although he doubted his old colleague Steve Jenkins had changed that much in the past few years. By the time he was *let go* by the police, he was way too far down the rabbit hole of conspiracy theories to look back. He did everything he could to avoid being digitally registered anywhere and even refused to receive his pension, as that would mean *they* would still be watching his every move.

While completing his half-hearted online search, Peter fondly remembered their time working together as constables. Back then, there were no signs of the paranoia that would later dominate Steve's life. Before his two divorces and far too many murder enquiries, he had been fun to work with, and with youth on their side, they had worked and played hard together. Steve's vague interest in popular conspiracy theories had started after he transferred to the Met. They had stayed in contact with one another and initially met up regularly. Over time, the meetings became less frequent, and Steve's failing grip on reality was more marked with each visit. Peter didn't want to consider that Steve might not even be alive.

As young constables, they immediately bonded over their mistrust of Jack Harris, a DS back then. Over the years, Steve had said lots of things that were best forgotten, but one of his obsessions was his belief that Harris was employed by the agency. He never clarified who exactly the agency was, but he took a keen interest in monitoring Harris. If Harris had any dealings with Rob Lewis in the past, on or off the record, Steve would know about it.

Steve's last letter had come from an address in Ladock. There were probably numerous villages around the country with that name, as well as the one on the outskirts of Crowcombe, but Peter's gut told him that was where he would find him. Whether anything he said would make any sense was another matter.

Peter had worked his way through half of the storage boxes in the attic when he found his old address book. He flicked through the pages and came to the rough sketch Steve had drawn showing where to find his home in Ladock if Peter ever fancied a visit. After comparing it to Google Maps, he was sure he had the right village. Stiff from crawling around in the attic, he headed outside to his car.

CHAPTER THIRTY-SIX

Peter expected Steve's home to be similar to Chris's stable block, so he was surprised to arrive outside an unremarkable two-bedroom bungalow. It was off the beaten track along a farm driveway, so perhaps Steve relied on the normalcy of its appearance, as much as its location, to give him anonymity.

As he approached, Peter saw movement in a window, so he was sure someone was in. A battered Ford Fiesta was parked outside, but there was no answer when he knocked. He looked back at the decrepit car and doubted it was taxed and insured, let alone driveable. He knocked again and called out Steve's name. Finally, he heard someone approaching the door. The door opened a short way, and a thin, haunted face peered out. Steve quickly glanced at Peter before looking past him to the track. "Have you come alone?"

"Yes. Good to see you."

"Were you followed?"

"No. No one knows I'm here."

Steve opened the door and stepped back into the dark hallway. "Come in quickly and close the door behind you."

Inside, the bungalow was basically furnished. Despite the drawn curtains, there was enough light for Peter to see that everything was spotlessly clean, although his nose twitched at an overpowering stench of boiled cabbages or something similar.

"Would you like a coffee? I grow the beans myself. I only eat and drink my own produce because the government is putting drugs into everything," Steve said, leading Peter into a small living room.

"No, thanks. I'm fine," Peter said, sitting on a hard-backed chair, shocked by Steve's sickly appearance. They were the same age, but Steve's grey skin sagging on his underweight frame made him look much older. Taking in his appearance as his eyes adjusted to the gloom, Peter suspected he made his clothes as well as growing his food and rarely or never saw the light of day. Trying to keep his expression neutral, Peter asked, "How have you been keeping?" as if they had just bumped into one another in a supermarket.

"So-so. I need to keep my wits about me at all times," Steve said, with eyes darting around the darkened room. "You're quite sure you weren't followed. You're the only person I've ever told my whereabouts."

"Quite sure."

"I always knew you could never be corrupted. You were always too honest. But trusting. That's your weakness. It's good to see they haven't got to you. Do you need my help?"

"I'm after some information you might have." Peter cautiously added, "About DCI Jack Harris?

"Ah," Steve said, nodding his head. "I knew it. It was only a matter of time. I have several files on him. He's in it all, right up to his neck. What do you want to know?"

With a sinking heart, Peter kicked himself for thinking this was a good idea. Seeing his old friend's state of health was upsetting, and he couldn't rely on anything he said. And he'd had the brass neck to taunt Simon for relying on information from Dick. At least Dick had one foot in the real world. But as he couldn't think of anything else to say and as he had driven out here, he might as well ask, "Does he have a connection to Rob Lewis?"

"Rob Lewis, Rob Lewis," Steve muttered, pacing the room. "Rob Lewis." He stopped abruptly and turned to face Peter. "Yes. There was something a few years back. Rob Lewis. I'm sure that was his contact. Wait here. I'll go and check my notes. I know which file it will be in."

"That's great, thank you," Peter said, somewhere between

shocked and highly sceptical.

Steve turned in the doorway. "Cameras will be watching you, so stay put while I check the files."

Peter looked around the room, trying to spot the cameras. He couldn't see any, but that didn't mean there weren't any. Although there were no electrical items in the room, Steve would have state-of-the-art, untraceable computer equipment somewhere in the house. Sitting still and waiting was not his forte, but he had no choice. There was a good chance Steve would return with nothing or a load of useless mumbo-jumbo, but there was the slim possibility he would have something worthwhile. If he moved from the seat, no matter how innocently, there was a good chance he would be thrown out empty-handed. Thoughts of better uses of his time were growing stronger when Steve reappeared. "Did you find anything?"

"Possibly. Harris was left with egg on his face a few years back after a bungled investigation into what was believed to be an international ring of car thieves. High-value cars were being stolen and sold to waiting buyers in Cyprus. Harris was using it as a cover to have a series of other secret meetings, although he did meet with Rob Lewis regularly," Steve said, tapping his nose. "The case collapsed when it was proved in court that his intelligence was wrong. Other countries and agencies were involved, and his part in the debacle was embarrassing. I suspect Rob was being encouraged by others to be misleading. He was probably taking a cut from the sales and being paid handsomely. I could dig around a little more to see what else I can find."

"I can take it from here," Peter said. "Thanks for pointing me in the right direction."

"You should leave now before people realise that you're missing."

"Oh, okay," Peter said, preparing to leave. He was keen to check if there was a grain of truth in the story. Harris had always relied heavily on informants, and Rob's background made him a logical choice in a car theft case. Harris would hold a grudge if the case had existed and collapsed as Steve suggested. He always hated to look foolish. It could explain why he was so keen to charge Rob and discourage a wider investigation. "We should meet up again soon."

"Okay, but not here. I'll contact you with a location. Wait until you hear from me."

Peter looked back at the bungalow before getting into his car, remembering why he had stopped staying in contact. He wished there was something he could do to bring his old friend back to reality. But what? Steve was way past the help of a friend. Maybe if he had acted years sooner, professionals could have done something to anchor him in the real world. Another regret to bury with all the others.

CHAPTER THIRTY-SEVEN

Before starting the car, Peter saw he had a missed call from someone called Judy. Aware that Steve was probably watching from a window, and not wanting to increase his anxiety, he decided to drive a few miles before returning the call. After driving through the small hamlet of Ladock, he hit redial on the unknown number.

"Hi, it's Judy. Judy Keller. I live, or used to live, opposite Jane and Rob. You asked me to call if I heard anything. I spoke to my husband after you left, and he thinks he recognises the man walking the dog you mentioned."

"That's brilliant. I'm not far away, so I could swing past to speak to him."

"He's working away for a few days, so that won't be possible," Judy said. "But he's sure the man lives in the sheltered bungalows a few streets away from us. The street is called Cranleigh Crescent, and there are only ten bungalows, so he shouldn't be hard to find."

Peter looked up the address and decided to drive over there to check. It would take less than half an hour, and as it was sheltered housing, there was a good chance he would be in. If the man was a credible witness and could place Rob on the bench, along with evidence of bias of the senior officer leading the investigation, they were moving closer to securing Rob's release.

While he would love to show Jack Harris up, casting doubt on police procedure left Peter feeling conflicted. It wasn't the same as proving beyond any doubt that Rob was innocent. He hadn't sounded Simon out on moral ethics, but he didn't want to be responsible for releasing a guilty man.

His niggling doubts centred around Rob's possible financial gain; despite Simon's insistence that Rob wasn't financially minded, experience had taught Peter that everyone has a price. Or was that his jaded view of humanity again?

Simon had convinced himself from the start that Rob was innocent so he wouldn't experience Peter's dilemma. Not being able to see the contents of Jane's will was infuriating. If it were solely down to him, he would delay reaching any conclusions until the terms were revealed.

Peter mulled the case over as he drove. Against the possible financial gain, Rob's neighbours and friends thought him incapable of murder, and once the circumstantial evidence against him was removed, the case against him was weak.

The row of purpose-built bungalows in Cranleigh Crescent was easy to find. They had probably been built by the council in the sixties and, while ugly, would be spacious by modern standards with larger-than-average rear gardens. With no idea which home he was looking for, he parked outside number one and rang the doorbell. The occupant's daughter opened the door and instantly recognised the description Peter gave. "That's Stuart in number six. You're in luck as I just saw him wobble in from the pub, but you had better get your skates on. He'll be sleeping it off until he wakes up later and realises the dog hasn't had a walk."

Peter thanked her for her help and walked over to Stuart's house. It was identical to the others right down to the mown front lawn, which Peter put down to the council. The doorbell wasn't working, so Peter rapped on the door and called Stuart's name, which caused an excited patter of feet and high-pitched yapping from inside. It was followed by a gruff, "Quit your noise, or next door will be complaining again." Moments later, the door opened as far as the security chain would allow.

Peter explained who he was, handed his card through the small gap and stepped back to wait.

The card was passed out through the small gap. "What do you

want with me?"

"I believe you had words with a drunk on a bench a while back when you were walking your dog late at night," Peter said. "Can you confirm if I've got that right?"

"It's not a crime. If he said I touched him or his stuff, then he's a liar."

"Nobody is saying you did," Peter said. "Can I come in?"

"What for?"

"So you can tell me what happened."

"Nothing happened. The drunk idiot was leering at me when I was walking by minding my own business."

Peter scrolled through his phone. "If I showed you a photograph, would you recognise him?"

"Possibly. I'm not sure." Stuart took the phone when Peter held it up to the door. A few moments later, he handed it back. "Yeah, that's the lazy no-gooder."

"If I came in, could you give me a brief statement confirming that?"

The front door shut, and Peter was about to walk away when he heard the chain being slid across and the door reopening. "Come on in then, but make it quick before I change my mind. I haven't got all day."

Half an hour later, Peter walked out with a brief signed statement. Stuart would be an okay witness. Peter was in no doubt that if presented correctly, they had enough evidence to secure Rob's release from remand and possibly have the charges dropped. But niggling in the back of his mind was a voice saying that just because Rob was seen extremely drunk on the bench that night, that didn't mean he hadn't killed Jane.

He considered ringing Simon to update him and see how his enquiries were going but decided to leave it until later. Before speaking to Simon, he wanted to check that Steve was correct about the car theft debacle, Rob's part in it, and whether, by some miracle, the wills had arrived early.

CHAPTER THIRTY-EIGHT

Simon's head was pounding, and he was tempted to crawl back into bed after his meeting with Rob. Only his determination not to let Peter down again kept him going. Pouring himself another glass of water, he vowed to stop drinking to excess. He would learn how to say no after a couple of drinks. He had made the same promise numerous times before, but it would be different this time. He had noticed his hands shaking during Rob's interview, which frightened him.

As requested, he had pushed Rob hard, but little new came out of it. Rob had insisted that he never had more than the odd flutter on the Grand National; he only met Chris after he started dating Jane, and the name Daryl meant nothing to him. He wasn't surprised to hear someone had beaten Chris up and had no interest in his injuries.

Rob claimed to have spoken to Jane several times to try to stop her meetings with Chris, but only because they upset her. She had always replied it was a family matter that didn't concern him, so he had let the matter drop. If he had known Chris was likely to turn violent, he would have made more of an effort. Jane had told him there was a trust fund, and he had never questioned its existence because he considered her finances to be her business.

Rob vaguely recalled Jane telling him that she was seeing a new firm of solicitors, but he had assumed she was thinking of changing her employers. A letter confirming their meeting was sent after the police had taken him in, and Lucy had opened it. Until then, Rob didn't even know Jane had a will, let alone that he was a beneficiary. It wasn't something they had ever discussed. All he knew was that Lucy had dealt with it on his behalf.

Simon worried he was being naïve, but he believed Rob. Despite everything he knew about his inheritance from his first wife, Simon didn't see Rob as the sort of person to be overly concerned with money. And if he didn't know about Jane's wealth, it wasn't a motive for killing her.

Simon mulled over his suspicion that Jane and Chris were involved in some sort of money-making scheme. While that could explain both attacks, nothing suggested any such business existed. Despite the lack of evidence, Simon liked the idea, as Rob was in custody when Chris was attacked, putting him in the clear.

Simon looked at the list of names the journalist had given Peter. Could one of them be the murderer? After his encounter with Daryl's friend, he wasn't keen to contact them. When he did, he had no intention of going alone to meet them, so they would have to wait until later.

He decided to contact Rob's solicitors for an update and ask for a list of things taken from Jane's home.

"Hi, Simon. It's good to hear from you. Everything is going well this end," Ed said. "There is a list somewhere. Do you want me to send it to you? Liz is back from her break and has read through all the evidence. She doesn't think that the police have grounds to hold Rob on remand and will formally request his release today."

"Brilliant. Let me know how that goes," Simon said, hiding his frustration that it hadn't been done before. "And if you could email the list to me, that would be great. Also, did you know that Jane's brother is in hospital after being attacked?"

"No, I didn't. Do you know what happened?"

"Only that he was found badly beaten in a pub garden after it closed," Simon said. "It's possible his attack was connected to Jane's murder, and neither had anything to do with Rob. We're going to do some digging around over the next couple of days. If we find evidence of a direct connection, will that be enough to force them to drop all the charges against Rob?"

"Liz will decide on that, but added to the solely circumstantial evidence the police have, I think there's a good chance of it," Ed said.

"Thanks," Simon said. "Before I go, there is one more thing. Rob seemed to think Jane was seeing a firm of solicitors to apply for a new job. Do you know anything about that?"

The phone went quiet for a while. "No, but are you sure it was about a new job? I've been trying to get a copy of Jane's will for the file, but her solicitor keeps stalling. The last time I called, I spoke to a junior secretary. She looked at the file and said the delay was because of the possibility of a newer will with another firm."

"Interesting," Simon said. "Can you follow up on that? Today."

"I'll try again, but so far, I've been met by a wall of silence," Ed said. "I'll e-mail the police list over to you now."

When the email arrived, it showed that the police had concentrated on going through Rob's things and had taken little notice of Jane's, which gave Simon an idea. A copy of the new will or something that indicated Chris and Jane had a joint financial venture could still be in the house, and it was time to show some initiative. Instead of discussing the possibility with Peter, he rang Lucy to get the key to the house.

CHAPTER THIRTY-NINE

An hour later, Simon inserted the key in the door of Jane's house with high hopes, and his headache forgotten. If the police had gone in with a blinkered vision, solely looking for evidence to support Rob's guilt, they probably missed all sorts of useful information. Lucy told him that Jane was meticulous about keeping her paperwork in order. She stored everything in the box bedroom upstairs, which she used as an office when she occasionally worked from home.

Lucy had been correct about Jane's meticulous record-keeping. A row of storage boxes was stacked along the back wall of the tiny room. In them, Simon found bank statements and household bills in date order going back for years. Another box was full of guarantees and warranties for every electrical appliance she had ever bought and all the instructions and care leaflets. At the bottom, he found details of her investments and savings in an unlabelled box. He sat on the floor and started to sift through the statements. Jane had been extremely lucky or shrewd and had died a very wealthy woman.

Simon sat back and wondered how the police could have missed all the paperwork spread out around him. The only explanation was that they weren't looking because they had decided Rob was guilty before they started their investigation.

Jane had the amount of money people would kill for. While it had taken him a while to find the box under everything else, it wasn't locked away. Could he believe Rob had never had a rummage through out of curiosity and found what he had seen?

From his cross-legged position on the floor, he looked around the room. He had opened all the boxes, but none had contained anything to suggest she had joint dealings of any description with her brother. He also hadn't found a will, which he thought surprising for such an organised person. Even if she didn't have a copy of the new will, the old one should be about somewhere. The only place he hadn't looked was through the drawers of her desk.

Her laptop had been taken by the police, leaving behind only a pile of legal textbooks on the desk. He flipped through them to confirm they were what they appeared to be. He tugged at the first drawer to find it was locked. It took him seconds to discover the key, stuck underneath the desk with a blob of blue tack. The first drawer contained the usual paraphernalia of stationery and random bits and bobs. He pulled out the contents of the second drawer to check through them, but they were all related to her employment. In the third and final drawer, he discovered her will. After pulling it out, he felt all around the drawer to check nothing else was in there.

He made himself comfortable in the office chair to read the contents. Before starting, he flicked to the signatures at the end. He didn't recognise the names, but the will had been drawn up and signed nearly two years ago, and her intentions were clear. Small amounts were to go to various charities, and a generous lump sum, enough to buy a modest house, was to go to Lucy. The remainder of the estate was to be split equally between Rob and Chris.

The chair creaked as Simon leaned back to look around the room. There was no way to be sure, but if someone had gone through the room's contents before him, they had gone to great lengths to put everything back to how they found it - everything except anything relating to a joint business venture with Chris and her updated will. He pulled out his phone to call Peter.

CHAPTER FORTY

Peter whistled when he saw the size of Jane's estate. "It's an amount worth killing for, but until we see the contents of Jane's updated will, we don't know who was going to gain or lose out."

"My money is on Chris being written out," Simon said. "That makes the most logical sense."

"Possibly, but we can't rule out the possibility that Jane was going to end her relationship with Rob. The little we've found out about her suggests she was pedantic and played everything close to her chest. Admittedly, she received a generous inheritance, but she made her fortune through shrewd financial decisions. In her mind, the practical first step in ending a relationship could be addressing the financial situation."

"That's cold," Simon said.

"Everyone is different," Peter said, shrugging.

"Was it all down to her judgement and luck, or could someone have been giving her financial advice? Inside knowledge, possibly?" Simon asked.

"An interesting thought, but did you find anything to support it?"

"No, but that doesn't mean she wasn't meeting up with someone."

"It's something worth bearing in mind, but without any paper records, it would be hard to prove. You could recheck her phone records, but I don't think you'll find anything," Peter said. "For now, let's focus on Rob."

"Who had no idea that Jane was so wealthy or that he was in her will."

"For argument's sake, let's just say he did." Peter took Simon's shrug as an agreement and continued, "We know there was an increase in arguments, and Rob was drifting back to hanging out and drinking with old friends. Jane may have been thinking about ending things for months, plucking up the courage to tell Rob she wanted him out of her life and the house."

"Are you saying that's what they argued about that night rather than Rob arriving home drunk?"

"I wasn't, but it makes sense," Peter said, nodding his head encouragingly.

"No, it doesn't," Simon said. "Why have the argument in the house? Why not wait until they were in the restaurant to discuss it, assuming that was her plan? With an audience, the conversation was less likely to become heated."

"True, but Jane was a very private person," Peter said. "Or maybe that was the plan, but her hand was forced. She complained about Rob turning up late and drunk, and things spiralled from there."

"You've been determined to find Rob guilty from the start," Simon complained. "Just as we have enough to get him released, you come up with this."

"It's one possibility that's worth pursuing," Peter said. "I don't want to be responsible for releasing a guilty man."

"I don't think he is," Simon said.

"Okay, so where do we go from here?" Peter said to calm things down. "Shall we go through our reasoning for suspecting Chris?"

"He's been unpleasant and violent since he was a child, he has a massive chip on his shoulder about Jane's inheritance and a whole host of other things, he's an alcoholic gambler in debt and his only alibi is a horse. What more do you need?"

"I don't disagree with any of that," Peter said. "Did you chase the police for the traffic footage?"

"Sorry, I forgot. I'll get onto it."

"In answer to your question, that's what I need. Some evidence that Chris left his sick horse and drove to his sister's that night."

Simon fell silent while he returned the will and other documents he had taken from the house to a folder. "Women generally discuss their relationships with friends, especially if they're failing and Jane didn't mention anything to her work colleagues, Clemmie and Caron."

Peter rubbed his face. "I think we made a mistake there. We were so keen to go and find Chris that day, we interviewed them together. Separately, they might have said more, especially if one of them thought Jane had shared personal details only with them."

"It's not that late," Simon said. "If it will erase your doubts about Rob so we can focus on Chris, we should speak to them this evening."

"I think we'll have to," Peter said. "My doubts could be satisfied in an instant if Foxfields would release details of Jane's final will. I accept that their hands are tied by probate rules, but they could hint at what the change was. This is a murder enquiry."

"Oh, didn't I say earlier," Simon said. "Jane instructed a new firm to write up her will."

"Seriously? No, you didn't," Peter said, thinking that was the first thing he should have mentioned. Scrabbling for a pen, he asked, "Do you have their details?"

"No, and I don't know for sure a new will exists," Simon admitted, before repeating his conversation with Ed. "Jane had also mentioned new solicitors to Rob, but he thought she was considering changing jobs."

Peter groaned. "These new solicitors are probably the ones who wrote to Lucy, and she's already said she threw their letters into the bin."

"She might remember the name if we pushed her a little harder," Simon suggested.

Battling to contain his annoyance with Foxfields withholding vital information in the hope no one would discover the second firm of solicitors, Peter finally said, "If you contact Clemmie and Caron, I'll call Lucy."

CHAPTER FORTY-ONE

When Simon called Caron, she was rushing around preparing for a date night with her husband. "Sorry, I'm dishing up tea for the children, and I still need to have a quick tidy-up and get myself ready before the babysitter arrives. What did you say again?"

"Did you chat with Jane about relationship issues? Any problems she was having with Rob?"

"Not in any great depth, no. We would share the usual moans about lack of support and being untidy around the house, but nothing specific."

"Did she recently complain about Rob's drinking and reconnecting with old friends?"

"She talked to Clemmie more than me about things like that. Sorry, I can't help you, and I really do need to get ready to go out."

"Okay. Thanks for your time. I hope you have a good evening." Simon looked up to see Peter ending his call and preparing to leave. "I take it you had more luck than me?"

"I'm on my way over to see Lucy. She thinks she wrote down the solicitor's name somewhere. She'll look for it while I drive over there. If she doesn't find it, I hope I can jog her memory by talking her through the letter's contents and the conversation she had with them. I'll press her again on why she failed to mention the solicitor's involvement from the start and see what she comes up with. And the fact she is going to receive enough money to buy her first home."

"She might not have known," Simon said. "Rob had no knowledge of the will."

"So he says. And I thought he told you that Lucy had dealt with everything. Something doesn't add up," Peter said. "Anyway, I had better get going. I'll ring you later with an update."

Simon watched Peter leave, looked up Clemmie's number, and crossed his fingers, hoping for a better result.

"Hang on a minute, I've just arrived home," Clemmie said. After clattering around, she said, "What can I help you with?"

"We're trying to find out more about the state of Jane's relationship with Rob just before her death. Did she say anything to you about it? In private, maybe? Something you didn't want to say in front of Caron?"

"Not really."

"She never said anything to suggest she was considering ending the relationship?"

"No, that was never the impression I had. I mean, she was worried about him drinking too much and some of the people he was hanging out with, but she was more concerned than annoyed. That's the way I read it, anyway. When we talked, it was more along the lines of how she could improve things. You know, get through to him that if there was a problem, she wanted to help. That sort of thing."

"Jane thought Rob had problems?"

"She had noticed he was drinking more, and she wondered why," Clemmie said. "The last time we spoke, she talked about getting away for a bit."

"By herself?"

"No, together, just the two of them. I think she had more of a romantic break in mind," Clemmie said. "So, in answer to your earlier question, I don't think she had any intention of ending the relationship - not without a fight, anyway."

"Okay, thanks, that's super helpful to know." Simon ended the call and checked the time. Kate would be home soon. If he got a move on, he could walk the dogs, get rid of the take-out boxes and empty beer cans, and have something cooking for her when she walked in. He left a message for Peter saying Jane was planning a romantic holiday and had no intention of breaking up with Rob, before locking up the office and heading home.

CHAPTER FORTY-TWO

When Albert and Alfred alerted Simon to Kate's arrival by their excited barking, the house was tidy, and a fruity chickpea curry was bubbling away on the stove, nearly ready to serve. He checked himself in the mirror and was pleased to see there were no outward signs he had been quietly hammering his liver to death in her absence. He forced his face into a happy smile and went outside to meet the campervan and help Kate carry her overnight bags.

The dogs shot past him as soon as the van door creaked open. They were in the van, climbing all over Kate before she could move from her seat. While Kate laughed, hugging the dogs in turn, Popeye jumped out of the van, sniffed, and trotted into the farmhouse, doing the dog equivalent of an eye roll.

"Enough, boys. Let Kate out," Simon said, holding the door open. "Did you have a good time?"

"Quiet," Kate said, pushing herself out past the dogs. "I'll grab my bags, and you can tell me what you've been up to."

"Missing you, mostly," Simon said. "I'll take your bags. Are you hungry?"

"Starving," Kate said, passing out her bags. "Are you going to suggest the pub?"

"No," Simon said, feigning a hurt look. "My special fruity curry is ready whenever you are. But now you've mentioned it, shall we pop down the pub after?"

Swinging her backpack onto her shoulder while Simon picked up the other two bags, Kate said, "I'm tired. Can we leave the pub for another night?"

"Sure," Simon said, leading the way into the house. "Give me a shout when you're ready to eat."

Over dinner and a bottle of wine, Kate told Simon about the animals she had been looking after and then asked how he was. Simon ran through their progress on Rob's case to divert attention away from himself.

"Who do you think killed Jane?" Kate asked.

"I thought for a while that Chris and Jane had some dodgy business arrangement, and Chris was attacked by the same person who killed her. But now I'm convinced Chris killed her because she was changing her will to leave everything to Rob. I think she was going to tell Rob that night about it and the holiday she was planning. A real shame that they argued, and she didn't get the chance."

"Has Peter come around to your way of thinking?"

"He's wavering. He thought Jane might have been planning to end the relationship, but I've just put that theory to bed."

"Have you seen a copy of this new will?"

"Not yet, but Peter is trying to discover more tonight. I'm confident that we'll have Rob free by tomorrow teatime."

"If the will says what you think it does," Kate said. "How sure are you of her intentions?"

"It's the only thing that makes sense. Chris hopes that under the terms of the old will, he will receive everything if Rob is found guilty. That's why he accused him of the murder. To think, I almost felt sorry for him being beaten up."

Kate furrowed her brow. "Did Chris know about the new will?"

"I don't see how he could have done. Even Rob didn't know anything about it," Simon said, recalling their first conversation with Chris and his assumptions about how Jane was going to change her will to favour Rob. Had he seen the new will? "But thinking about it, maybe he did. I should let Peter know."

"And are you still friends with Peter?"

"Yes," Simon said, sounding offended. "Why wouldn't I be?"

Kate laughed. "Okay, Sherlock. It sounds like you have it all figured out, and you look exhausted. You can call Peter in the morning. Let's go on up to bed. We can sort the dirty plates in the morning."

CHAPTER FORTY-THREE

Simon and Kate were chatting in bed the following morning when Simon's phone rang. Simon said, "Leave it to ring," when Kate reached over to pick it up and read the screen.

Kate handed over the phone, "It's Peter. You probably should answer it."

Simon sighed but accepted the call. "What? Now? Okay, I'll be five minutes," Simon said, swinging himself out of bed. "Peter is on his way over. The solicitor who prepared Jane's new will is prepared to speak to us. It has to be now, as he's in court all day and will be for the next few weeks."

"You'll soon know if your theory about the will's contents is correct," Kate said. "And it leaves me to do the dishes, feed the dogs and walk them."

Pulling on a shirt, Simon said, "Sorry."

"You can make up for it tonight. Off you go. You don't want to keep your new best friend waiting."

Simon picked up a pillow that had been kicked off the bed in the night and threw it at Kate. "I'll see you later."

Simon managed a slurp of coffee before Peter's car arriving set the dogs barking. He poured the rest of the coffee into a travel mug, did his best to settle the dogs and hurried out to meet Peter. Jumping into the passenger seat, he said, "I take it Lucy was able to remember the name after some persuasion."

"Not exactly," Peter said, turning the car around. "She was as vague as before, but she remembered where they were based when I pushed her. I found them online and rang them first thing this morning."

Early rush hour traffic slowed them down, but they arrived at the solicitors with a couple of minutes to spare. A tall, angular man in an expensive suit and shiny shoes met them at the entrance and introduced himself as Jasper Powell. "There's a decent coffee shop between here and the courts. We'll talk there."

Settled around the table, Jasper said, "I've agreed to chat with you as you already know the contents of the will."

Peter carefully said, "We know the contents of the previous will held by Foxfields."

"Then you know the details of the will we wrote for Jane. It was essentially the same," Jasper said. "On her first visit, she brought a copy of her original will and explained she wanted the terms to remain the same. On the afternoon of her death, she came in to read through what we had prepared and say whether she was happy with it."

"And was she happy with it?" Peter asked.

"Yes," Jasper said. "She took it away to read it through again and sign it."

"On the afternoon of her death, she definitely had the updated will in her possession?" Simon queried.

Jasper nodded. "She left with the new will and her copy of the old one."

"I assume she had fallen out with the previous solicitors," Peter said. "Did she say why?"

"It wasn't so much a falling out as she had more faith in the range of financial services we provide. To put it politely, she didn't think her boyfriend and her brother would know the best way to handle receiving a large sum of money. While the terms remained unchanged, she wanted us to handle the money on their behalf. As I explained to her, we can only strongly advise how clients spend their money, but we would do our best as it would be in our interest to be retained as fund managers."

"I see," Peter said. "But there was no change to how the money would be split? The bulk of the estate was to be split equally between Chris and Rob with a lump sum going to Lucy."

"Yes, that was her wish. Obviously, there is an issue if Rob is found guilty of murder, but we sent letters to all the beneficiaries advising them of the new will and urging them to recognise it. We haven't received a response yet, and we understand Foxfields continue to act as if they hold the last will and testament. Conveniently, no one knows the whereabouts of the will we prepared. If the will was signed and witnessed that afternoon, then the matter is clear cut."

"So, the dispute is about which firm handles the matter, not the contents of the wills," Peter said.

"Correct. Other than an increase in the estate's total value, the details are almost identical," Jasper said. "If you are in contact with the beneficiaries, can I urge you to ask them to consider the superior service we can provide?" He produced two glossy brochures from his briefcase and handed them a copy each. "Please take your time to read through the services we provide and call me if you have any questions. I'll leave you to enjoy your drinks in peace."

"I don't suppose we could have a copy of the will you drew up?" Simon asked.

"Not until probate is settled, but you have my word that the contents are broadly the same as in the will your colleague has already seen. If there's nothing else, I really must go."

"There is one thing," Peter said. "On the afternoon Jane came to see you, was there any sense of urgency?"

Jasper looked confused before Peter asked, "Did Jane indicate her life was in danger? Like her death was going to be sooner rather than later."

Jasper shook his head and picked up his suitcase. "No, nothing like that. People of all ages like to have their will in order for all sorts of reasons. Peace of mind, generally, in case the unexpected happens."

"Wait a minute," Simon said. "When did you contact Chris Forbes?"

"Several weeks ago. We've chased him for a reply but have not heard anything back."

"His home isn't registered as such," Peter said. "Who gave you his address?"

"Jane did."

"There's a chance he hasn't received your correspondence," Peter said. "Have you tried to ring him?"

"We would if we had his number," Jasper said. "If you know how to reach him, could you ask him to contact us?"

After Jasper left, Simon flicked through the brochure.

"There goes your theory that Chris killed her because she was writing him out of the will," Peter said.

"The same applies to Rob," Simon said. "Neither of them had more reason to kill her than previously."

"Unless Rob wanted to end the relationship," Peter said. "I'm livid about how Foxfields have been so unhelpful, in the hope they would retain the business. Surely, there's a code of conduct covering this sort of situation. I might lodge a complaint."

"When we first met Chris, he thought his sister was going to write him out of her will. His ungrounded fears gave him a motive for the murder," Simon said. "I suspect he still hasn't received their letter."

Peter sighed, and said, "Chris must have some way of receiving his post. Maybe he uses a post office box."

"I can't imagine he's too concerned about bills not reaching him," Simon said. "When it comes to his motive for killing Jane, nothing has changed."

"That's one possibility, but we can't discount Rob," Peter said. "Jane may have been keen to save the relationship with a romantic holiday, but it doesn't necessarily follow that he felt the same way."

"There you go again, trying to prove what we've been asked to disprove. He didn't know anything about the will," Simon said, before sighing and picking up his coffee.

"We're talking about a considerable sum of money, and I'm considering all the possibilities," Peter said. "Although I do agree Chris seems the more capable of the two of murder."

"Now you're talking," Simon said approvingly, putting down his coffee mug. "We press on with searching for any recent, large debts he has."

Peter pushed his empty coffee cup to one side. "I'm trying to understand how and why Jane would have kept her wealth secret from Rob. Maybe she didn't completely trust him and wanted to be sure he loved her for herself."

"That doesn't mean anything other than she had self-esteem issues stemming from her childhood," Simon said. "And her brother did nothing to boost her self-image."

"True," Peter said, "I know you're convinced it was Chris, but I've got a horrid feeling we're going around in circles missing something. Although, I'm damned if I know what it is."

CHAPTER FORTY-FOUR

Peter and Simon walked back to the car, deep in thought. They had both pinned their hopes on the changes in Jane's final will giving a clear motive for murder.

Peter climbed into the car and looked across at Simon. "I wonder if Chris is feeling any better. Let's pay him another visit. We might be able to drag something more out of him."

"It will be interesting to see his reaction when we tell him that his sister had no intention of disinheriting him," Simon said. "He lost his temper and killed her for nothing."

Arriving at the hospital, they learned Chris had been moved from the side room to a ward. Luck was on their side as they couldn't see the nurse who had previously limited their time with him. Not wanting to push their luck in case she was only on a break, they quickly moved to his bedside.

Chris shut down whatever he was looking at on his phone before they walked in, but Peter thought he recognised the betting logo from the brief glimpse he caught. The bruising had come out, so his face looked worse despite a slight reduction in swelling, but Chris looked far more alert.

Simon stood at the foot of the bed while Peter pulled out a chair from beside the bed and sat. "You're looking much better."

"It looks a lot worse than it is," Chris said. "I'm waiting to see if I'll be discharged later today."

"Has your memory of the attack returned?" Peter asked.

"No. The doctors say it's common after a traumatic experience never to remember the details, so you're wasting your time here."

"I'll be the judge of that," Peter said. "And anyway, we've come to give you some good news. I assume you want to hear it."

"Go on," Chris said suspiciously.

"We've just spoken to the solicitors Jane visited on the afternoon of her death. You'll be pleased to know that after expenses and a few bequests, she still wanted the balance of her estate to be split equally between you and Rob."

Chris made a strange gurgling sound and turned his head away, hiding his expression. "Give me a moment, please." His eyes were watery when he turned to face them again. "I should have had more faith in her. Her decision might bring me some comfort in the future, but could you leave now so I can grieve in peace."

"I'm sure the money will help soothe your pain," Simon said. "And clear your debts. How much do you owe Daryl?"

Chris looked like Simon had just slapped him across the face. "I don't know what you're talking about."

"Are you concerned he might come back to finish you off? Was killing your sister a warning for you to pay up?"

Chris went white and looked down.

"Or did you tell him your sister could easily settle your debts?" Simon asked.

"No. I would never … Where did you hear that?"

"Things like that don't stay a secret. How did Daryl know where your sister lived if you didn't tell him?"

"He could have looked it up, the same as anyone could," Chris said.

"So, you do owe him money," Simon persisted.

"I'm a sick man. Stop twisting things around and confusing me," Chris said, still looking down. "I have a head injury, and it's hard enough for me to think straight as it is."

"You do owe him money, though, don't you," Simon continued.

"Okay, yes, but …"

"And you mentioned your sister to him," Simon said, pleased with himself for forcing Chris to admit that he knew Daryl.

Chris hesitated, focusing all his attention on the hospital

blanket. He looked up, and said, "I feel terrible, but I think I let it slip that she controlled my money once."

Peter flashed Simon a look telling him to back off. In a softer tone, he asked Chris, "Is it possible when you couldn't pay, he decided to go to her to collect the money you owed?"

Chris looked away, refusing to answer.

"You never thought to mention this before, although you were quite happy to accuse Rob of killing your sister for her money?" Simon asked.

"That seemed the most likely explanation before."

"Before what?" Simon asked.

"Before you started to make wild accusations about Daryl," Chris said. "I have no idea who attacked me. I'm absolutely gutted by your suggestion there could be a connection to my sister's death and would appreciate some privacy."

"Murder isn't a private matter," Simon said.

"You're telling me," Chris said, drawing his knees up to his chin under the blankets.

Peter flashed Simon another warning, and asked, "Can you remember anything about the night you were attacked? Who you were with earlier on, perhaps?"

"No, nothing," Chris said. "It's a complete blank."

"Do you mind telling us how much you owe Daryl?" Peter asked.

"A bit."

"Hundreds? Thousands?"

"Thousands," Chris reluctantly told Peter.

"Is that why you killed your sister?" Simon asked, unable to contain himself any longer.

"What? No way," Chris said. "Who are you? I thought you were gathering evidence about Rob for the police."

"To get your hands on the money to pay off your debts? That's why you went around to see her that evening, and she refused," Simon said, hoping he could now goad Chris into admitting to the murder.

"No. I would never do something like that."

"Like you told us you had learned your lesson and no longer gambled money you don't have. Like you quickly moved from blaming Rob to blaming Daryl. You killed your sister. Why don't you admit it?"

Instead of answering, Chris looked past Simon and called, "Nurse! Nurse!" When the nurse came over, he told her he wasn't feeling too good and wanted his visitors to leave.

Peter pulled Simon away. "We were just leaving."

Simon gave Chris a final look of disgust and marched off.

Peter caught up with Simon in the hospital corridor. "You were a bit harsh back there, weren't you?"

"Because I don't believe a word he said. He brutally stabbed his sister to death in a fit of temper."

"I'm not sure about that, but we might have gotten more from him if you had been less abrasive," Peter said. Sighing, he added, "I agree he probably accused Rob in the hope he would receive all his sister's money."

"Did you see how guilty he looked when you told him Jane was still leaving half her money to him? And how quickly he shifted to accusing Daryl?"

"It's possible the men who beat him up were connected to Daryl if he owes him money," Peter said.

"He probably owes lots of people money."

"We could visit the pub at lunchtime to see if the landlord remembers anything. He might be more forthcoming as we're not the police, but I don't see how much it would help us other than maybe make you feel less guilty."

"I'll live," Simon said, dismissing the idea. "There's another way we could check on his finances."

"Go on."

"We could pop around his home while he's still in here."

"Breaking and entering would be illegal," Peter said. "And I don't fancy our chances with those dogs."

"Luckily, I have a plan."

CHAPTER FORTY-FIVE

In the car, Simon pulled out his phone and, looking very pleased with himself, he found the number he needed. "Hi, Ted. It's Simon. Remember me? I'm a mutual friend of Chris. I called you before to ask you to take care of the dogs and ponies."

"Ah, yes. I remember now," a gruff voice replied.

"Well, good news. They should be letting Chris out of the hospital soon, so he'll need a change of clothes. I'm not going to lie, I'm a little scared of his dogs. I was wondering if you could meet us at the house and if you could walk them while I pack up a few things for Chris."

After a long silence, Ted said, "I'll meet you outside his place with a change of clothes in half an hour," and hung up.

Peter couldn't help laughing. "Well, come on then. We had better get over there and collect these clothes. It might at least give us another chance to speak to Chris. He might have calmed down by the time we return."

"I bet it would have worked if we were in a movie," Simon said. Despite his disappointment, he couldn't help but laugh at himself, which dispersed some of the tension that had been building between them. He struck a pose and added. "Ryan Gosling could play me."

Peter looked across quizzically. "I could see you in Barbie land."

After pulling a fake horrified look. Simon asked, "Which actor would portray you?"

"Someone suave, sophisticated and incredibly good-looking," Peter replied, equally keen to improve the atmosphere between them.

"And modest. Don't forget modest," Simon said. "So come on.

Which actor?"

"Maybe a young Sean Connery. Or the actor my daughter likes. James McAvoy."

They remained in good humour, although at times it was a little forced until they reached the layby. Before leaving the car, Peter said, "I hope the dogs are locked inside and not roaming their territory while Chris is in the hospital."

"We're a little early," Simon said. Do you want to wait a few minutes so we can be sure Ted is already here dealing with the dogs?"

"No. He said he would have the clothes ready within half an hour, so he's probably already inside. Let's start walking. I don't want to waste all day on this."

A mud-splattered truck with oversized tyres, abandoned rather than parked outside the stable block, proved Peter correct. As they approached, a man in stained farm overalls, who they assumed was Ted, walked out of the end stable carrying a key and a handful of dog biscuits. "Hi," Peter shouted. "We're here to collect the change of clothes."

"You nearly gave me a heart attack, creeping up on me like that," Ted grumbled. "If you're not keen on the dogs, I suggest you wait in my truck."

"Can't we come in with you?" Simon asked, starting to follow him towards the house.

Ted stopped and abruptly turned so he was nearly nose-to-nose with Simon. "No."

Simon drifted back towards Peter as Ted marched across the yard to the front door. He opened it and threw a handful of dog biscuits behind him. While the dogs were wolfing down the treats in the yard, he slipped inside the house, closing the door behind him. Once the treats were gone, the dogs turned their attention to Peter and Simon, who quickly decided they would seek sanctuary inside the truck after all.

Ten minutes later, Ted reappeared at the front door carrying a plastic bag. He called the dogs and threw the remaining biscuits inside the house. After they rushed past him to find the treats, he closed the front door behind them. He handed the bag to Simon once they had climbed out of the truck and waited for them to walk away.

While driving to the hospital, Peter asked, "Why are you so sure that Rob is innocent?"

"I've told you I don't think he's the type to be influenced by wealth or even seek it. He comes across to me as more of a free spirit, unconcerned with material things. His daughter and friends insist he's not a violent person, and if he had killed Jane, why did he return to the house so early that morning? He knew his daughter wasn't due back until the end of the weekend. Wouldn't he have given himself more time to destroy any evidence? He was too drunk the night before to do anything."

"Killing someone can have a very sobering effect," Peter said.

"The state he was in after leaving the pub, I don't think he could have made it that far. And if he'd killed her earlier in the evening, don't you think after destroying all the evidence, he would have created a better alibi than getting blind drunk in his local and collapsing on a bench?"

Peter would agree that Rob couldn't have done it if it hadn't been for the two windfalls. Could he really be so unlucky in love yet lucky with money?

Back at the hospital, they walked directly to the ward, where they found Chris asleep on his bed. As they neared the bed, a nurse hurried over to shoo them away. "Please don't disturb him again. He took a turn for the worse after your last visit."

"Sorry to hear that," Peter said. "We understood he was going to be discharged later today."

"Not now, he isn't. He'll be stopping here a while so we can keep an eye on him."

Simon held up the plastic bag. "We brought him a change of clothes."

The nurse took the bag. "I'll put it in his side cabinet, but I must ask you to leave."

"Okay, sure," Simon said, following the nurse. "We're sorry we upset him earlier. I am worried about him. He lives alone and doesn't take great care of his health. If I gave you my number, would you let me know if there's any change in his condition?"

"If I'm on shift, I will," the nurse said, taking Simon's number.

Simon caught up with Peter in the corridor. "That was a waste of time," he complained as they left the hospital. "We didn't even get to speak to him again."

"Never mind. Think of it as your good deed for the day," Peter said, leading the way to the car. After starting the car, he asked, "When you spoke to Rob's solicitor, did he say whether they've made any progress?"

"The lead solicitor is back, and she's formally requesting his release."

After hesitating, Peter said, "I spoke to Rob's neighbours, and they all agreed he was a pleasant guy. While I was there, I tracked down the man walking his dog that night. He's made a statement confirming he saw Rob drunk on the bench. Also, DCI Harris might have reasons to hold a grudge against Rob. I won't know for sure until I speak to Rob again, but it's possible he was a police informant in the past. Meanwhile, can you send the statement from the dogwalker to Ed?"

"Will do. I'll call him now to let him know it's on its way," Simon said. "Hey, do you fancy coming over to meet Kate later? Hopefully, we'll be celebrating Rob's release."

CHAPTER FORTY-SIX

Peter had been nervous about how the evening would go. But when he turned up outside Holly Bush Farm clutching a bottle of wine and a box of chocolates, Kate made him feel immediately welcome. The conversation over an excellent home-cooked meal was light and entertaining, and by the time they moved into the living room to finish their drinks, Peter felt mellow and at ease.

Kate was refilling glasses when Simon's phone rang. From Simon's side of the conversation, it was obvious that the solicitors were calling with a mixture of good and bad news.

"Don't keep us in suspense," Kate said as soon as the call ended. "Will I have good news for Charlie when I collect him from the airport?"

"Partly," Simon said. "Rob was released home earlier this evening."

"I sense there's a but," Peter said.

Simon nodded. "He's been released on bail pending further enquiries, but Rob isn't satisfied. He wants all the charges against him dropped and his name cleared. They think he will probably contact us for more help."

"Won't they drop the charges, anyway?" Kate asked, retaking her seat. "From what you told me earlier, the case against him lacked any hard evidence from the start. It sounds more like they are trying to save face."

Before Simon could reply, his phone rang again. Checking the screen, he mouthed, "Rob." Ending the call, he said, "Did you get the gist of that? Rob wants to instruct us to find out who really killed Jane. He doesn't have any faith in the police looking for alternatives. What do you think? I said I would get back to him."

"Is it something you have to run past Charlie?" Peter asked.

"No, we can make the decision, but anyway, this is more of an extension than a new case," Simon said. "We're already nearly there with proving it was Chris."

"I'm not so sure," Kate said. "Charlie always deals with the details, but I think you should ask for payment for securing Rob's release and then open a new case."

"Whatever," Simon said. "You agree with me now, don't you, Peter? That the most likely suspect is Chris."

"Possibly," Peter said. "Although if Jane wasn't going to dramatically change her will to favour Rob, he doesn't have a strong motive."

"Chris didn't know that," Simon said. "And if the will wasn't the defining factor, maybe the amount he owed Daryl and the vet's bill was. Chris visited Jane that evening asking for help with the bill, and she turned him down."

"Do we have street footage to confirm that?" Peter asked.

"I think the police finally sent it, but I haven't been through it yet," Simon admitted. "Half the time the cameras aren't working properly, anyway."

"That's what we'll be doing tomorrow morning." Peter sighed. "But bear in mind that the horse had already been treated, so it wasn't urgent. A night dash to see his sister wasn't needed."

Simon groaned and was about to comment, when Kate said, "The will is still central to everything." Kate looked between Simon and Peter and added, "Otherwise, the killer wouldn't have taken it that night."

"How do we know it was taken that night?" Simon asked.

"Everything else was still neatly stored in her office, wasn't it?" Peter asked Simon, catching on to what Kate was saying. "Other than the will's absence, was there anything to suggest someone had been rooting through her paperwork?"

"Everything was neat and tidy in the back room," Simon said. "But we know several of the other rooms were searched."

"Are you quite sure the police didn't take the will?" Kate asked.

"Yes, I've been through the list of items taken several times, and there's no mention of it," Peter said.

"I'm only going on what Simon has told me," Kate said. "But if Jane visited the solicitors that day and planned to tell Rob that night, she would have had the will ready to show him. She would have had it in her bag or somewhere to hand, like on a counter or tabletop."

"Okay, so Rob is in the clear as the police searched him at the scene," Simon said.

"At the scene, maybe," Peter said. "But he would have had plenty of time to destroy or hide it."

"Brilliant, Kate," Simon said, ignoring Peter's comment. "You've been on board for five minutes, and you've confirmed Jane's death was related to the contents of that will." Simon looked at Peter. "I think Chris took it. We must search his house while he's still in hospital."

"We've discussed this already. On what grounds? Apart from the lack of any evidence he was at the house that night, the will's terms were unchanged, and he was already used to his sister controlling the purse strings. I agree he's obnoxious, but where's his motive?" Peter asked. "It's just as possible that the will is what Jane and Rob argued about that night. It had nothing to do with him arriving home the worse for wear. He didn't like the idea of the money being tied up and under the solicitor's control. Or maybe it was the first he had heard of it, and he didn't want to share half of it with Chris."

"Except, the solicitor admitted they couldn't insist they retained control; they could only advise," Simon pointed out.

"What Jane told him is more important. She may have chosen to tell him differently, hoping he wouldn't later question it," Peter said. "Also, you keep insisting that Rob didn't even know a will existed. If that's true for Rob, then it's probably true for Chris."

"Except on our first visit, he thought Jane was about to change the terms of her will," Simon said, his voice becoming louder and shriller. "That could mean he did know. Or that he was lying to make it look that way."

"Either way," Kate said. "When Jane changed the terms, she would discuss the matter with her boyfriend before updating a brother, who you say she didn't get along with."

"True," Simon admitted, slumping in his chair. "How come every time we discover something, you use it to make Rob look more guilty than innocent?"

"It's about weighing possibilities," Peter said. "But Kate is right. I can understand Jane wanting to talk through her intentions with Rob that night, but not with Chris. Why would she?"

Simon glared at Peter. "You've wanted him to be guilty from the start."

"All I've ever said is I want to discover the truth about what happened that night," Peter replied.

"Why don't we leave it there for the night?" Kate quickly suggested. "Let's not ruin a lovely evening arguing over something that may or may not have happened."

"Agreed. We should look at this with cool heads tomorrow," Peter said, shocked by how quickly things had escalated from where he told Simon he couldn't break in to go through someone's personal possessions for no reason. He was only stating the obvious. Even if they found something, how would they explain finding it? Chris could claim they broke in and planted it. Surely, Simon understood about operating within the law. "My taxi should be here soon. I can wait for them outside."

"If you're sure. It's been lovely to meet you." Kate said, nudging Simon to say something.

Simon put his glass down and stood. "How about we meet in the office at ten to thrash things out before I call Rob? We can't take his money if we're going to be trying to prove his guilt."

"That seems reasonable. It will give me time to check what, if anything, the street cameras picked up. I'll see you at ten." Peter went to shake hands, but Simon had already walked away. He shrugged and gave Kate an it's-okay smile before seeing himself out.

Kate waited until she heard the taxi leave before moving to the kitchen to tidy things away. She was frustrated by how the evening had ended. Simon could be so infuriating at times. It was hardly surprising he had so few close friends. He pointlessly alienated and eventually fell out with everyone, and his mood swings were becoming worse. She didn't know what to say to him anymore. She knew something was bothering him, but every time she asked, he denied it. She stiffened when she heard Simon enter the kitchen.

"What are you doing out here?"

"I don't want to leave all this until the morning," Kate said, continuing to load the dishwasher with her back to Simon.

"Anything I can do to help?"

"I'm almost finished in here. You could wipe down the dining room table," Kate suggested. She didn't want to be in the same room while she sorted out her feelings and was relieved to see him obediently heading towards the dining room. There had to be a way to get through to Simon how rude and stubborn he sounded without it being a drama. She wished she could think of a way to broach the subject without sounding overcritical. Simon wasn't a bad person. He could be caring and compassionate when it suited him, so why was he being such a jerk?

Kate looked out over the dark garden and tried to remember when the friction had started between Simon and Charlie. Initially, they had worked well together. Only in the last few months did the ribbing start to have more of an edge. If only Simon would say what the problem was instead of hoarding everything inside. Bottling up everything was at the bottom of it all. He had never dealt properly with the grief of losing his family. She jumped when Simon reappeared directly behind her. "All done?"

"Yes," Simon said, putting an empty glass on the side. He stood in the middle of the room, looking awkward. "Sorry. Did I mess up your perfect meal?"

Kate shrugged, not sure what to say. She didn't want him to turn it around to make it all about her. "A little, but don't worry about it."

"I didn't mean to sound so abrupt. I used to be good with people. Now ..." Simon ended the conversation with a little boy's look of helplessness.

"It happens," Kate said, moving towards Simon. That look of his always worked on her. "I thought you liked Peter. Do you want to talk about it?"

Simon put on his mask of a lopsided grin. "Another time. I need to set my alarm clock as I want to be up early tomorrow. I'm sure you agree that I need all the beauty sleep I can get."

"Why? You aren't meeting Peter until ten o'clock."

"All part of my plan. I'm going to get a head start. There's something that proves only Chris could be the killer and I'm going to find it before I meet Peter tomorrow."

"It's not a competition," Kate said wearily.

"I know, but it will save Peter from wasting time looking at the camera footage for answers, and we can present the evidence to the police together," Simon said. "I know I'm right."

CHAPTER FORTY-SEVEN

Simon slid carefully out of bed so as not to disturb Kate. He lingered by the bed. It wasn't often that he was the first one up, and she looked so beautiful when she slept - so beautiful he thought he might make it a habit to wake up early, just so he could watch her for a while before going back to sleep.

He quickly turned away. The problem with habits is that they become difficult to break. Eventually, she would tire of him like everyone else. Then he would have to wake up to look at an empty pillow. Anyway, he was too busy for such sentimentality. He had things to do. He quickly dressed, told the dogs to look after Kate, made a coffee to go and quietly closed the front door behind him.

The sky was cloudless, but he shivered in the early morning chill, while the heavy dew seeped through his trainers as he walked to his car. He switched on the car heating and turned out of the driveway. He relaxed in the car seat, confident that soon he would have all the proof he needed to prove he was right. As the heating warmed his damp feet, he kicked himself for not grabbing his wellingtons on the way out. Admitting that oversight allowed other doubts to creep into his mind.

He pushed his lingering qualms away. Recently, he had become too cautious. As long as he believed he would succeed, he would. His positive thinking had always carried him through before. It was better than overthinking every small detail. Concentrate on the bigger picture and leave the details to fall into place in their own time.

When he parked in the muddy layby, he was full of optimism. The sun rose in the sky, vaporising the dew as it dried. He whistled as he set off up the track, listening to a woodpecker working in the trees above him. He searched the branches but couldn't see the bird. It fascinated him that something so small could make so much noise.

Before he knew it, he was outside the stable block. When they collected the clothes, Ted had emerged from the nearest stable, so he was sure that was where he would find the key. He felt along the beam over the stable door, and sure enough, there it was. He slipped it into his back pocket and checked the row of dustbins. The first two contained horse feed, but as he expected, the third was filled to the brim with dog biscuits. He filled his front pockets with them and headed across the yard toward the makeshift house.

His nerves reappeared when he heard the snarls and barks coming from inside. He slowed his breathing to mask his fear and reached into his back pocket for the key. He placed it in the lock before pulling out a handful of treats ready to throw, as soon as the dogs barrelled out the door. He would be safely behind the door before the dogs realised that they had failed to protect the house from a stranger. A stranger determined to see their owner behind bars for murder.

Standing to one side, Simon turned the key and eased the door open, simultaneously throwing a handful of dog biscuits into the yard. One dog raced through the open gap, not paying any attention to who had opened the door. The second hesitated and looked directly at Simon. "Good boy," Simon said, doing his best to sound confident and threw another biscuit. The dog looked at the biscuit and back at Simon, his upper lip quivering as it considered whether to growl or pounce. His attention was broken by the other dog turning to snatch up the biscuit. Torn between ripping Simon to shreds and fighting for the biscuit, the dog wavered before running through the doorway. Simon threw another handful of treats and quickly slipped inside, slamming the door behind him.

CHAPTER FORTY-EIGHT

Inside, Simon leaned against the door to catch his breath. He was safe with all his limbs intact. Worrying about how he would leave the house and reach his car in one piece was a problem for the future. Now, he had to concentrate on finding Jane's will. He moved quickly through the living room, checking the drawers filled with race cards. Empty-handed, he moved half-filled mugs of mouldy coffee to check through piles of old newspapers and racing form books scattered on every available surface. He looked behind cushions, finding a grey pair of discarded underpants. Trying not to wonder how the pants had found their way there, he looked under the furniture, discovering months of dust, a sock and an empty cigarette packet.

He straightened up and looked around the room for a possible hiding place he hadn't yet searched. Seeing nothing, he told himself not to worry. Chris was hardly likely to leave incriminating evidence hanging around where a casual visitor could see it. The thought of Chris entertaining almost made him laugh out loud. He put it down to his nerves and tried to relax.

The will was most likely hidden somewhere private, like in his bedroom. But time was on his side, and rushing the search would be foolish. It was best to move through the house methodically. He would search the kitchen next and then concentrate on the bedroom.

He searched every drawer and cupboard in the kitchen and checked inside the cooker, bread bin and fridge. Ignoring the smell of rancid, gone-off scraps, he searched through the bin.

Telling himself not to feel despondent, he accepted that the will wasn't in the kitchen.

He had a quick look in the bathroom. The only place anything could be hidden was the bathroom cabinet, but that contained nothing more than headache and indigestion tablets. He withdrew to the hallway and approached the bedroom door, confident that was where his search would end.

Compared to the rest of the house, which was far from tidy, the bedroom was a filthy mess. The room smelled damp and sour. Every surface, from the windowsills to the small bedside cabinet, was covered with a thick layer of dust. Dirty fingerprints blackened the light switch. Even the elaborate display of cobwebs was weighed down with dust. On the bed was a dirty, scrunched-up bedsheet tangled with an assortment of discarded clothes and a half-eaten sandwich. The only thing of value in the room was the wide-screen television mounted on the wall.

Simon tentatively picked through the surface debris before turning his attention to the bedside cabinet. It contained only a couple of sticky glasses and a whisky bottle. Ignoring the barking dogs outside and a growing sense of failure, Simon opened the wardrobe door. It was rammed with clothes, but only those on the right-hand side were free of dust. Additional jumpers and sweatshirts were packed tightly on a shelf above the hanging area. An assortment of shoes littered the base of the wardrobe. And there, under a battered pair of boots with broken laces, was a large brown envelope.

He pulled it out and turned it over. It was addressed to Jane Forbes. He almost forgot himself and sat on the bed to read the contents. Thinking better of it, he blocked out the noise of the barking dogs outside and carried the envelope back to the living room.

Sitting well out of reach of the offending pair of underpants, he pulled out Jane's two wills and started to read the most recent. The contents were as the solicitor said, but the point was he now had proof that Chris had murdered his sister. It was the only explanation for it being there. All he had to do was work out how to leave the house and return to his car safely. There was no rear door. The only way out was back the way he had come. He could only hope the dogs weren't bored of the trick with the treats.

As he had proved his point, he considered calling Peter for help before remembering how scared he was of the dogs. Dick might be a better bet. At least the dogs had stopped barking so he could think straight. Maybe they had become bored and had wandered off somewhere so he could slip away without them noticing.

Simon was returning the document to its envelope when he heard the key turn in the lock. He jumped up and looked desperately for somewhere to hide. Not that it would help if the dogs came in. They would sniff him out straight away. He shoved the envelope under his sweatshirt and turned to face the door.

"What the hell are you doing in here?"

CHAPTER FORTY-NINE

Peter let himself into the office and switched on the coffee machine. He would appreciate an apology from Simon for last night, but he would settle for them finalising matters without an uncomfortable atmosphere between them. He wouldn't be rushing back to work with Simon again. He might be intelligent and quick, but he was also tetchy and far too temperamental for the type of work.

His back and eyes ached from watching the grainy video footage that had finally turned up from the police. The first thing he had done was check that it covered all three of the routes Chris could have taken to Jane's home. Although it often yielded good results, it was a job nobody liked, and one he had always delegated to junior officers in the past. His eyes were as grainy as the footage, but he persevered while he waited for Simon.

There were no cameras in any of the streets surrounding Jane's home. That would have been far too simple, but all three routes would have taken Chris past cameras at some point. After watching the footage covering the most direct route through the town centre and the quickest route via the ring road, he decided to break for another coffee before checking the final route. He stretched his arms above his head and noticed the time.

He called Simon's mobile while he waited for the coffee machine to finish. When he received no answer, he tried the landline, and Kate answered after a few rings. "Hi. Is Simon there?"

"Simon? No. He left hours ago."

"Hours ago?" Peter queried. "We agreed to meet at ten."

"He said something about getting a head start. He left here just after seven."

"I've been here since before nine, and nothing suggests he's been here. Did he actually say he was coming into the office?" Peter asked, thinking he should check whether any major car accidents had been reported.

"I assumed that was what he meant, but no. He didn't specifically say that was where he was heading."

"Can you remember what he said?"

"Something about he was going to find evidence that proved Chris killed his sister," Kate said. "I assumed he meant he was going to go back through the files to see if anything had been missed."

"I'm being pedantic here, but did he say he was going to find evidence or *the* evidence?"

"Sorry. I'm not sure."

"Okay. No need to worry," Peter said. "I have a good idea where he is."

"Should I be worried?"

"No. I'll head out to find him. As soon as I do, I'll tell him to ring you."

Peter sat in front of his laptop and took a deep breath, determined to enjoy his coffee before going in search of Simon. He knew where he was and was annoyed with himself for not anticipating it. In the unlikely event he did find the will or any other evidence at the house, any solicitor would have a field day. Simon wasn't stupid, so what part of inadmissible evidence did he not get?

Kate said Simon left at around seven. Even if he had hit early morning traffic and couldn't find what he was looking for in the house, he should be on his way back. Despite what he'd said to reassure Kate, he decided to finish going through the road footage. There were only two cameras on the scenic route Chris could have taken. If, when he finished watching them, he still hadn't heard from Simon, he would start worrying.

Peter sped the footage to the time he wanted and squinted at the screen as he sipped his coffee. His vision was blurred by his eyes watering, and he angrily wiped them. He didn't need glasses. What he needed was a break from searching for a vehicle that wasn't there. He stopped the video and walked around the small office.

Ten minutes later, he returned to his laptop and hit play. He immediately hit pause. Damn. He looked closer at the image and magnified the number plate. He leaned back in his chair. There was no doubt it was the vehicle he was looking for.

While it wasn't enough to say Chris had visited Jane that night, he was heading in that direction and had lied about staying home all evening. It would have been enough to persuade the police to request a warrant to search the house. With Simon's fingerprints all over the property, that was now a complete waste of time. It would be too easy to argue that he planted any evidence found there.

Chances were that the idiot was already on his way back, with or without the will. While driving out would calm his irritation, he would likely miss Simon travelling in the opposite direction. Even if he caught him still searching the house, the dogs would be loose outside and becoming bored, making him an easy target. If Simon answered his phone now, Peter knew he would tear him to shreds and say some things he might later regret. His last coffee had gone cold, so he decided to make another in the hope that the delay would take the edge off his anger.

When he returned to his desk with a fresh cup, the office phone rang. Peter snatched it up, expecting it to be Simon, but it was a woman who spoke.

"Hi. Is Simon Morris there? He's not answering his mobile."

"No, but I can take a message," Peter said through gritted teeth.

"It's Sue from Crowcombe Hospital. He asked to be kept updated on his brother's progress."

"Oh yes," Peter said. "And how is he?"

"That's why I'm calling. He discharged himself earlier this morning. I wondered if Simon had seen him," Sue said. "We're worried about him, and I wondered if Simon could pop over to check on his brother."

"I'm sure he could," Peter muttered, putting down his mug. "What time did he leave?"

"Before I came on shift at nine. Someone thinks they saw him getting into a taxi shortly before eight."

"Thanks," Peter said, taking a slurp of coffee and picking up his car keys.

CHAPTER FIFTY

"I thought you were in the hospital," Simon lamely said, unable to think of anything else to say. His mind was too busy working overtime, trying to invent an innocent excuse for why he was there.

"Obviously," Chris replied. "Why are you snooping about my house? And how did you get in past the dogs?"

Averting his eyes from the shotgun, Chris casually held at his side, Simon said, "I've always been good with dogs."

"Not these dogs. One word from me, and you'll be torn to shreds. It will be a heartbreaking story. I returned home to find my dogs had made their own breakfast arrangements. I'll probably need counselling, the cost of which I'll claim back from the police." Chris gave a hollow laugh. "We can discuss how my childhood damaged me and made me who I am."

Simon swallowed. "Where are the dogs now?"

"In the hallway, waiting to be fed," Chris said. "What were you hoping to find here?"

"Here?" Simon asked, his brain scrambling for ideas. "Here. Well, I'm on your side. I was hoping to find something that might incriminate Daryl. Some evidence that he was threatening you and your family over unpaid debts."

"Why would you want to do that?"

"Because, well. Umm. We've been looking for an excuse to bring him in for some time and ..."

"Are you even with the police?" Chris asked, pulling out his mobile phone with his free hand. "Simon something or other, wasn't it? If I call the station, will they vouch for you?"

"DI Ford will know who I am, but let's talk about Daryl. He's a nasty piece of work, isn't he? I met one of his friends the other day. Big chap with fat fingers and a knife. Wears a flat cap. Do you know him?"

"Ah. So, I have you to thank for the rumour that I've been badmouthing Daryl."

"I didn't say anything of the sort," Simon said. "But you do know him, then?"

"Possibly, but I'm not stupid. I have no intention of accusing Daryl of anything. Why do you think I would? And why do you care, anyway?"

"Don't you want to know who killed your sister?"

"You're not with the police, are you," Chris said, still holding his phone. "So, what's your interest? I can always call them to ask."

"Okay, okay. You've got me. I'll come clean," Simon said. "I'm a friend of Rob's. He didn't kill your sister, but he wants to know who did. I had an interesting chat with a friend of Daryl's the afternoon before you were attacked. I'm convinced he killed Jane, and I was hoping to find some evidence of that and him attacking you. The last I heard, you were going to be in hospital for some time, and they wouldn't let me speak to you. You can call the hospital to check. I came back to ask you for permission, but they sent me away. I dropped off a change of clothes for you. Did they tell you?"

"They did. Ted said you looked dodgy and not to be trusted."

Simon smiled and shrugged. "It's my face, what can I say?"

"You can start by showing me what you shoved under your sweatshirt."

"Umm ... I..."

Chris slipped his phone into his back pocket and raised his gun. "Come on. You may as well get this over with. There's no need to draw it out."

Sweat trickled down Simon's back as he slowly pulled out the brown envelope. "I haven't looked at it. I've no idea what is inside."

"But you've seen who it's addressed to."

"I assumed it was something from ages ago. Maybe from when

your parents passed."

"Is that so? When do you think I was born? Yesterday? You didn't come here to find evidence against Daryl," Chris said, stepping back and reaching for the door handle. "Rob sent you here to find evidence against me."

"No, wait. That's not true," Simon said as his heart rate rose at the thought of being torn apart by two hungry dogs. "It's Daryl I'm interested in. Let's talk."

"What's there to talk about? How I miss Jane? I do, you know. She was the only person who never gave up on me," Chris said sadly, turning the door handle. "I didn't want any of this to happen, but you've forced my hand."

"Tell me what happened," Simon said. "It's not like I'm going to be able to tell anyone else, is it?"

CHAPTER FIFTY-ONE

Peter switched his phone to hands-free as he sped towards Tidworth. He tried to call Simon again, telling himself there were plenty of other explanations for his disappearance. There was an outside chance that Simon had left the house before Chris arrived home, that he had heard him arrive and had snuck out the back, or that Chris was the first to arrive and Simon never went in at all. He was probably over-optimistic, but he kept an eye on traffic travelling in the opposite direction while waiting for Simon to answer his call.

Accepting that Simon wasn't answering, he stepped harder on the accelerator and called Crowcombe station. Traffic was lighter than he had expected, and he was making good progress. He estimated he should be outside Chris' home in less than twenty minutes unless he met any later snarl-ups. His call was finally answered, and he asked for DI Ford, only to be told he was out on a call and not expected back until midday.

"Could I speak to someone else who has been involved in the Jane Forbes murder case, then?"

"Can I ask what your interest is, sir?"

Swerving back onto his side of the road after overtaking a truck, Peter said, "This is an urgent matter. I need to be put through to someone familiar with the case now."

"Can I ask what makes it so urgent, sir?"

Peter wanted to scream but calmly said, "A friend is in danger. I believe he has been caught unaware in a suspect's house. You need to send officers around there before it's too late."

"I can send a squad car, sir. Could you give me the address?"

Increasing his speed, Peter explained it wasn't a registered address but gave directions on how to find the house.

"Thank you, sir. Now, if I could take your full name and address."

Peter gave his details, swearing under his breath as he took the corner too fast, causing a squeal of brakes.

"Sir, are you driving? It's an offence to use a mobile phone while …"

"The householder is armed with a shotgun and has two large, aggressive dogs. You need to dispatch the armed response unit and dog handlers. Once you've confirmed you have done that, I would be happy to slow down. And I'm using a hands-free set."

"Thank you, sir. Would you like to stay on the line until I confirm a unit has been dispatched?"

"If that makes you happy. Just do it now. It's a matter of life and death." Peter slammed on the brakes, nearly missing the turn for the village.

"Okay, sir. Hold the line."

Peter was forced to slow down in the winding lanes and stop to allow a couple of horse riders to pass. He accelerated down the hill, past Chris and Jane's childhood home and skidded off the lane onto the narrow track as the jobsworth at Crowcombe station confirmed an armed response team and dog handlers were on their way. He parked behind Simon's car in the layby, grabbed his phone, and started to run up the track.

He slowed his pace when the stable blocks came into sight. Everything seemed quiet in the house, and the dogs were not loose in the yard as far as he could see. Neither was the old truck, but that was probably still wherever Chris had parked it the evening he was attacked. Hope rose in his chest. Maybe Chris went to collect his truck first and had been held up because it had been clamped or towed away. He ducked into the stable block to update the police while watching the house. He was pompously told to return to his car and leave the area, so he ended the call.

He heard the dogs barking when he arrived, but there wasn't any sign of movement inside the house, and he was tempted to creep over to peek through a window. He wouldn't be popular, but he could at least cancel the request for an armed response team if Chris hadn't arrived home yet.

Standing in an empty stable was stupid if Chris was elsewhere, and he was becoming impatient doing nothing after the mad dash to reach the place. The dogs would start barking again if he approached, but they would go crazy when the officers arrived. It could quickly become a siege situation if Chris was in there with Simon. If he calmly knocked on the door, saying he was looking for his partner, would that create the opportunity for Simon to escape or inflame the situation?

Peter decided to test the dogs' reaction by throwing a stone towards the front door while remaining hidden inside the stable block. If Chris came to the door to investigate, he would at least know that he was there. If Simon had hidden when he heard Chris arrive, it might allow him to escape.

He threw the stone so it landed about a metre from the front door and waited. The dogs started barking immediately, and Peter realised he hadn't thought things through. What would he do if Chris sent the dogs out to investigate where the noise had come from? He stood perfectly still, watching for any sign of movement inside the house. His heart leapt up to his mouth, and he dropped to the floor when a shotgun went off.

CHAPTER FIFTY-TWO

Chris asked, "Does anyone know you're here?" Chris asked.

"No, no one," Simon replied, regretting not letting anyone know where he was going. Peter would have talked him out of it, giving him a long lecture on the correct procedure, but he could have told Kate.

"Not even the guy you came here with before?"

"Definitely not. He's an ex-copper and thinks everything should be done by the book."

"Wife or girlfriend? Or boyfriend?"

Simon shook his head. "My girlfriend is away house-sitting, so no one. We've all the time in the world. If you want to get anything off your chest to someone who isn't going to be able to tell - then I'm your man."

"Is she pretty?"

"My girlfriend?" Simon asked, momentarily thrown. "Yes, and kind and thoughtful."

"Are you planning to marry her?"

"One day."

"Well, there's your first lesson, lad. Never wait for one day. It often never arrives. In your case, it certainly won't."

Simon bristled at Chris handing him advice, especially as it looked like he wouldn't be able to act on it. "Point taken," he said, swallowing hard. "Shame I'll never put that lesson into practice. Do you want to tell me about Jane?"

"Do you like a whisky? I think you're a single malt type. Am I right?"

"Spot on," Simon lied, a people-pleaser to the end.

Keeping a careful eye on Simon, Chris walked backwards to a

side cabinet and pulled out a bottle of Loch Lomond and two tumblers. Never relinquishing the gun, setting them on the low table took two trips. His eyes bored into Simon as he poured out two glasses. "I'm not an easy person to like. I get that. Probably why I've never had a special someone."

"Never say never," Simon said. He was trying to sound optimistic, but it came out as patronising and mocking.

"I'm not interested in your platitudes," Chris snapped. "Can't say as I'm interested in anything you have to say, but only one of us is leaving here alive, and I would like to explain about Jane. As you so kindly offered, why don't you shut up and listen?"

"Okay, sure. Whatever," Simon said, picking up a glass. "Cheers."

Chris sat in his armchair with his shotgun and stared into his glass. "Our parents were beyond odd. They belonged in a long-gone period. Mostly, we learned from their example. We were taught that pride, arrogance, self-reliance and a thick skin were all we needed. We didn't need friends or fun. We were above all that. And if we fell short - let's just say we didn't like sitting down for a week. Talking of which, why are you still standing? Sit!"

Simon quickly dropped into the nearest chair, spilling some of his whisky. He looked up, but Chris wasn't paying him any attention. He was staring into space with a wistful look on his face. He looked vulnerable despite the shotgun.

"Jane somehow got past all that and made something of her life. But she never forgot and never gave up on me. Even when everyone else did, including myself. It's a disease, you know? Gambling. It's not something you can switch on and off."

"There are people who can help you with that."

"I thought I told you I'm not interested in anything you have to say. And anyhow, I was forced to try it once. It was useless." Chris gulped a mouthful of whisky and fell silent, leaving Simon to listen to the ticking of a clock while trying to look at anything but the shotgun.

CHAPTER FIFTY-THREE

Simon sipped his drink and watched Chris for a while, wondering how drunk he would have to be before becoming incapable of firing the gun. Once any hospital painkillers were factored in, it shouldn't take long. Then, he would just have to work out how to get past the dogs without harming them. The longer he could keep Chris chatting, the better. "What happened that night when the vet came to treat your horse?"

"The vet. Yes, it all started with her," Chris said, snapping to attention. "Sanctimonious little cow looking down on me. Scolding me like I was a child when she was half my age. It was all her fault."

"What did she do? I thought she treated the horse."

"That night, yes," Chris said. "But all those horses out there are rescue cases. Not one of them would be alive if it weren't for me. About half of them need a constant supply of drugs to keep them healthy and pain-free. One of them has Cushing's, and without her daily medication, she would be dead within a week. Another has asthma attacks, so I need an emergency supply of steroids. I could go on, but you get my point. She said the practice would stop supplying the drugs until I settled my account in full. Vets used to care about animal welfare. Now, it's all about profits That's why I had to visit Jane that night."

"I agree with you about the direction veterinary practice is going," Simon said, seeing an opportunity to drag out the conversation. "Large companies, run purely for profit are buying out small practices, so they have a monopoly in the area. Then, they can charge whatever they like. Some say they work hand in hand with the insurance companies. It's the animals that will suffer. And people like yourself. That's lovely, by the way. You rescuing horses. We have a little rescue dog called ..."

"I thought I said I wasn't interested in your pathetic little life," Chris snapped.

Chris topped up his whisky glass twice while ranting about the vet's unreasonable behaviour. Simon continued to take small sips of his whisky, nodding in all the right places while remaining silent.

"Anyway, I thought your last wish was to hear about that night," Chris said. "Because of that incompetent woman, I was already in a bad mood when I drove over to see Jane. I wanted to stay with Bobbie, but I needed those drugs for the others. It was like she was holding a pistol to their heads. Can you understand how that felt?"

"Absolutely. I would do anything for my dogs."

Chris gave Simon a withering look before continuing, "Jane took forever to answer the door and was dressed for bed when I arrived. She wanted me to come back in the morning, but I insisted we had it out there and then. I had to for the horses, but Jane kept stalling. Saying we could talk about it another day. That's when I saw it. The will on the side. And I knew that she was going to cut me off permanently and give everything to that dreadful bloke of hers. All that we meant to each other, everything we had been through, forgotten. She had moved on and wanted to leave me in the past. That's all I was. A sad reminder of a past she wanted to forget about."

Simon shifted in his seat, seeing how upset Chris was becoming. He couldn't be sure but thought he was close to tears. Reminding him that he was wrong about Jane's intentions would be like twisting a knife in his guts. He wanted to say something to make him feel better, but after his previous attempts, he decided to stay quiet.

Chris sloshed more whisky into his and Simon's glass, half of it ending up on the table. "Upset by the vet and desperate to settle that damn bill, I saw red. I lost it, struck out verbally, and said things I can never take back. I didn't mean any of it. It all came tumbling out of nowhere. I've heard people talking about a red mist descending. That's what it was like. I was out of control, but I'll never forget the hurt look on her face. I wanted to make it go away."

"Had you been drinking?" Simon asked.

"Some, I guess." Chris held up his glass and looked at it. "I suppose it didn't help. It wasn't really me. It was like I was possessed and not thinking clearly. I would never have said those things if I had been myself."

Simon risked quietly saying, "Diminished responsibility is a valid defence."

"To what?" Chris asked, sloshing whisky from his glass as he waved it about. "You're the same as everyone else. People always think the worst of me." Chris fell silent while he drank from his glass.

"Is that when you decided to take the will?" Simon asked.

Chris refilled their glasses, oblivious to how little Simon was drinking. "When it appeared, I wanted to destroy it. Tear it into shreds as though it never existed. I wish I had."

Simon started to shift his position, ready to make his move. Slipping forward in his seat, preparing to launch himself across the room, he asked, "Why?"

Chris was now heaving ugly sobs as he knocked back more whisky. "Because ... because I was wrong. She was still going to leave half to me." Sniffing, he pulled himself straighter in the chair and hardened his voice. "That doesn't mean she wouldn't have changed it in the future. But I swear to you. When I left, she was upset but alive and well."

Simon opened his mouth to speak and shut it again. After a moment's consideration, he decided that he didn't believe that last part. It was more likely that Chris had blanked out the part where he went crazy with the knife, stabbing her numerous times, but he saw the chance to drag out the conversation a little longer. The amount Chris was drinking would render him unconscious soon, so he could simply walk out the door and call someone. "Where did you find the wills?"

"I didn't find them. They appeared on the doorstep the following afternoon."

"How do you think they got there?" Simon asked, happy to play along with the fantasy if it improved his chance of escape.

"My blood turned cold when I worked it out. Rob killed my sister. He delivered them here to set me up. That's when I knew I had to get in first and tell the police it was Rob."

"Did you tell them about the wills?"

"How could I? They wouldn't have believed me. I don't know much about policing, but my fingerprints will be all over them. As they were in my possession, I would be the obvious suspect. If she had been planning to write me out, that devious snake would have left them at the scene. I've thought about this a lot. I didn't see him, but he must have seen me leaving that night. It's kept me up at night worrying that someone else might have seen me there, and it was only a matter of time before they told the police."

"If Rob saw you, why didn't he tell the police?"

"Because he's evil and cruel - like a cat playing with a mouse," Chris said. "It's his insurance policy. When the police find evidence to prove it was him, he'll suddenly remember seeing my car in the area to deflect attention from himself. If that doesn't happen, he'll use it to blackmail me. Heads he wins, tails I lose. He's not the nice guy people think he is."

They both turned when they heard the dogs barking and throwing themselves against the front door.

Chris jumped up, pointing the shotgun at Simon. "I thought you said that no one knew you were here."

"They don't."

Chris started to walk backwards towards the door. Halfway there, he lost his balance and lurched to his left. Simon jumped from his chair, hoping Chris was too drunk to react quickly enough to regain his balance. Chris steadied himself and raised the gun to retake his aim. Simon sprinted around the chair Chris had been using and charged, ploughing into Chris from the side and bringing him down. They crashed to the floor in a tangled heap, and the gun went off, creating a shower of plaster raining down on them. Rolling around the floor, Simon tried to wrench the gun away but was surprised to find Chris still had an iron grip on it.

CHAPTER FIFTY-FOUR

Peter shot across the yard and tried the door, only to find it locked. He banged on the door with his fists, shouting for attention. In between, he listened for sounds inside but could hear nothing over the excited barking. The door and frame were too solid for him to break in that way, so he sprinted around the building, looking for a window. He came to a small one around the back, and peering inside, he saw it was the kitchen. He was about to smash the window when he heard vehicle engine sounds. He retraced his steps to the front to see a police 4x4 bouncing along the track.

Four officers jumped out of the truck. Three started pulling equipment from the vehicle while one marched over to Peter. He started to explain the situation, but as soon as Peter mentioned the gunshot, despite his protests, he was dragged away from the house and forced into the back seat of the truck. He resented being called a civilian who was hampering their efforts. While it annoyed him, he accepted arguing would only further delay them, so he meekly sat quietly as requested. A moment later, a dog handler van, with two officers pulled alongside.

There was still no sound coming from the house except the constant barking. Feeling impotent, he could only sit and watch the officers discuss tactics as they donned protective gear.

The officers took forever checking and rechecking their equipment and setting up the loudhailer, and Peter became more fidgety by the second. As they had lost interest in him, he tried the door handle. As he suspected it was locked, but he doubted the front doors were. Keeping a watchful eye on the officers, he wedged himself between the two front seats so he could reach the front passenger door handle. He stretched as far as he could, which was just enough to pull the handle and push the door. It was unlocked. All he had to do was clamber over the seats without being seen, and he could creep away.

CHAPTER FIFTY-FIVE

Simon pulled and twisted but couldn't force Chris to let go of the shotgun. The best he could do was keep the gun pointing away. He questioned for how long - until one of them had a momentary loss of concentration? So far, Chris had astounded him in every way. What if it was his mind that wandered?

"You look surprised," Chris said with a crazy grin. "Did I tell you I built this place by myself, plank by plank? I discovered manual labour suited me. I've never been stronger or fitter."

Simon shouted for help from whoever had set the dogs off, but he doubted he could be heard over their barking. He hadn't heard anything, so he couldn't be sure there was someone outside. His first thought was that it was Ted coming to feed the dogs and horses, but he would have let the dogs out by now. Would the gunshot have sent him scurrying for cover rather than coming in to see what his friend was up to? And why hadn't he gone to the gym when Kate suggested it?

Chris started to writhe and roll about with renewed vigour. "Get off me!"

"Not until you let go of the gun," Simon said, forcing his mind back to the here and now.

"Like that's going to happen."

"It's over, Chris. Let go."

"Says who? Some puffed-up ex-public-school kid."

Simon nearly forgot himself and released his grip on the gun. He thought he had studiously lost all traces of his privileged childhood. His second thought was, why did he find it so important when he was rolling around the floor fighting for his life? But he couldn't resist saying, "Where I went to school is irrelevant."

"Boarding School?"

"How do you know?"

Chris tried a different tactic of twisting the gun and trying to head-butt Simon. Simon jerked to the side to avoid the impact, his hands slipping on the gun as Chris twisted the gun the other way. Simon tightened his grip and gave three hard tugs to no avail. They were evenly matched, which hurt Simon's pride as he had wrongly judged Chris to be overweight and going to seed.

Unless he came up with a new tactic, they could be locked together for hours, possibly until one of them became sleepy. Not a prospect he relished, but the dogs were safely outside in the hallway, and he had drunk a fraction of the whisky Chris had. He tried to knee Chris in the groin, but they were too closely entangled for him to create any power behind the movement. When Chris stopped trying to twist the gun from his grasp, Simon asked, "What gave me away?"

Breathing heavily, Chris replied, "I see parts of myself in you."

Appalled by the idea, Simon was quick to dismiss it. "Rubbish. You're just trying to get me to relax my guard."

"Oh yes," Chris taunted. "It's fine for other people. They have something to strive for. If only they had X, they could be all they wanted to be. But what if you've been given everything from the start? You've had every financial advantage and a private education but still feel like a failure, a useless freak? You could have been anything and had it all, but you end up a sad nobody. A figure of fun. Is that how you feel?"

Although he recognised some of those feelings, Simon shook his head and asked, "Is that how you see yourself?"

"Don't you?"

"No. Never. Whoever you're describing, it's not me."

"No? So, what are you doing with your life? What do you do other than trying to prove your vile friend's innocence?"

"I do plenty of other things, but how is that relevant? Right now, I'm trying to find out who killed your sister."

"Not me, for starters," Chris said. "Do you honestly think Rob is innocent? You haven't suspected at any point that he might be guilty? He's a drunk, by the way, but I expect you know that. Is that your poison? Your escape from underachievement?" Chris sniffed loudly. "Yes, I'm sure that's alcohol seeping from your pores."

"You're hardly one to judge."

Chris gave a hard tug on the gun, nearly wrenching it out of Simon's hands. "Let go."

"So you can shoot me?"

"No, so I can go and see who is out there."

"And let your dogs in to attack me? No way."

CHAPTER FIFTY-SIX

Peter managed to slither half between and half over the seats to land in a heap in the front passenger seat. He looked up to check that no one was interested in him. The officers all had their backs to him, either peering inside the dog handlers' van or crowded around the loudspeaker they had set up. He pushed the passenger door just wide enough to squeeze himself out of the car and quietly pushed it back so that it looked closed.

Crouching behind the truck, he peered around the corner. The distance to the house was short, but if he made a dash for it, someone would see him out of the corner of their eye if they didn't hear him. Keeping low, he shuffled himself to the rear of the truck. He could double back to the stables if he used the vehicle as a shield. From there, he could access the paddocks, follow the hedge line and hope there was a gateway or some other access behind the house.

He checked again to see if anyone was paying him any attention, and then ran the short distance to the stables. Pleased he hadn't been seen, he hurried around the back and climbed the fence into the paddock. One of the horses briefly raised its head from grazing before deciding he was less interesting than the next blade of grass. He ran along the hedge, careful not to stand on any fallen twigs and branches.

There was no gate to the house from the field, only a thick bramble hedge, but he spotted a small hunting gate to the adjacent field. Satisfied he couldn't force himself through the thick bramble, he dashed to the gate. It proved to be a good move as from that field, there was access to the rear of the house.

Unfortunately, there wasn't a door at the rear of the property.

Only the kitchen window he'd peered through before, which was far too small for him to climb through.

CHAPTER FIFTY-SEVEN

Chris and Simon halted their struggle for the gun when the phone rang, taking them both by surprise.

"Are you going to let me answer that?" Chris asked.

Simon glanced at the wall-mounted phone and back again. "We'll get up and walk over there together. I've never felt so attached to someone before."

Chris rolled his eyes at Simon. "Okay. We'll stand up on the count of three."

It took them several attempts to scramble to their feet while still holding tight to the gun, but eventually, they managed it. Slightly out of breath, they edged as one to the phone. Neither was prepared to release their hold on the gun to answer it.

"Now what?" Simon asked when the phone stopped ringing. A part of him wanted to laugh aloud at the ridiculous position they were in.

"Be quiet. I'm thinking," Chris said.

There was a loud crackling noise, and the sound surrounded them. "This is the police. Either you come out, or we will be breaking in. If your dogs aren't restrained, we will shoot to kill."

A roar came from somewhere deep inside Chris as he looped a foot behind Simon's and gave him a violent push. Simon felt the gun slip from his grasp as he fell backwards, hitting the back of his head on the concrete floor. He looked up, dazed, to see Chris rush to the door and pull his two dogs inside. The dogs growled at Simon but stayed close to Chris.

"No one is going to harm my dogs." Chris raised his chin and the gun, his eyes drilling into Simon's. "It seems only one of us is leaving here alive."

Simon staggered to his feet. Feeling dizzy, he steadied himself by holding onto the wall. "We could walk out together. You can explain how you found Jane's wills on your doorstep. I'll back you all the way."

Chris stood still with his eyes full of questioning. A look of childlike wonder took over his expression. Haltingly, he asked, "You believe me?"

A prickly sensation ran down Simon's spine, and he shivered. He couldn't tear his eyes away from Chris. "Yes. Yes, I do." Behind the words, Simon's mind was racing. If it wasn't Chris, then it must have been Rob. He had fooled them all, even his daughter.

Chris broke eye contact and jerked the gun, indicating Simon should move. "Outside. In the hallway."

Numbed and confused, Simon obeyed, not that he had an option. As Chris followed him out, he shut his dogs safely inside the living area.

The voice boomed from outside. "We'll try the phone one more time. If you don't answer or come out with your hands in the air where we can see them, we're coming in."

Chris pointed the gun at Simon as the phone started to ring. "Do you have dreams?"

Simon swallowed hard and said, "I ... I..."

"I used to have dreams," Chris said. "When I grew up, I was going to inherit the house and land from my parents and fill it with rescue animals. All the ones that other people didn't want because they were broken and scarred. Factory-raised chickens and pigs, broken down horses, betrayed and abandoned dogs and goats. I've always fancied goats. I wouldn't expect anything from them. They just had to be. That's what I wanted for myself. To be left alone to be me. Not much to ask, is it? People not wanting to fix me. I didn't mind people hating me. I liked it when they were frightened of me. It kept them away."

"You could still do all that if we walk out of here together," Simon said. "I'll help you to explain what really happened. I

215

think … we could even be … friends."

Chris threw back his head and laughed. "Much as I've enjoyed your company, we're not going anywhere together. No one is going to believe me."

"We'll make them."

Chris shook his head. "You know what they say about dreams?"

"No," Simon said hesitantly. Chris had muddled his brain. Why was he wittering away about dreams, and why had he shut the dogs in the other room?

"If you've got a dream, chase it - because a dream won't chase you back," Chris said before raising the gun.

"Don't you dare!" Realisation came crashing down, and Simon flung himself at Chris, reaching out for the gun. As they fell, the gun went off again, slipping to the side of Chris' jaw and firing into the ceiling, sending down a shower of timber this time.

Flinging the gun to the end of the hallway, rolling around on the floor while nose to nose with Chris again, Simon said, "We really should stop getting together like this."

The phone stopped ringing, and a loud crash came from the front door, sending the dogs inside the living room into a frenzy. Over the barking, Simon shouted, "We're unarmed, and the dogs are safely locked in another room."

Two officers hurtled through the forced door, closely followed by Peter. The first officer scooped up the shotgun and quickly handed it backwards to another waiting outside the door. Simon scrambled to his feet and backed away as Chris was hauled to his feet, handcuffed and cautioned.

Chris accepted the situation without a struggle until they tried to take him away. He stood his ground and turned to Simon. "Make sure the dogs are okay. They need feeding and settling down after all this upset."

"How do I do that without being eaten alive?"

"Talk to them softly and gently, and they'll be as docile as you like."

Simon looked doubtful. "I'll do my best. Once they're fed, I'll be right behind you. Tell the police what you told me. I'll be making a statement on your behalf."

"You really did believe me?" Chris asked doubtfully.

"Yes."

CHAPTER FIFTY-EIGHT

After Chris was led away, Simon took a deep breath and turned to face the living room. A part of himself he couldn't name or locate had shifted, and his thoughts were all over the place. Was he right to believe Chris, or was he blindsided by the situation and his obvious love of animals?

"You're not going in there, are you?" Peter asked. "There's a team of dog handlers out there. I'll go and get them."

In a daze, Simon slowly turned the door handle. "I believe him."

"Let's at least go and get some dog food and have the handlers on standby," Peter urged, nervously eyeing the door.

Simon let go of the door handle but remained facing it. Was he still harbouring doubts deep down? Chris was messed up inside and, before the police arrived, had been talking about setting his dogs on him. Was it a bluff, or had Chris truly intended to encourage his dogs to rip him to pieces at the time? There was a raw honesty in everything Chris said. And he was right about one thing - people wouldn't believe his story of how the wills came to be in his possession. Was that what Rob was relying on? He didn't understand why he hadn't said Chris was at the house from the start if he had seen him leaving.

Peter tapped him on the shoulder. "Simon?"

"Okay. We'll go and find their feed bowls." When Simon turned, the dog handlers were already approaching. He put his hands up to stop them. "I've spent some time with the dogs. They're fine."

"I'm going to collect their bowls," Peter said, disappearing along the corridor.

"Look son, I'm sure you mean well, but we're experienced with handling this sort of situation. With no one to take care of them, they'll need to be taken away anyway."

"No, wait," Simon said. He had made Chris a promise and was going to keep it. Worst case scenario, he would find a place for them on the farm. "Chris has a friend who looks after them when he's away. I can call him."

"What about long-term?"

"I'll arrange something."

Peter returned with a couple of bowls and tins of dog food, and after some more persuasion, the dog handlers relented. "We'll wait outside the door, and at the first sign of trouble, we'll take over."

Simon's knuckles turned white as he took a deep breath and stepped inside the room, gripping the two bowls. Both dogs eyed him suspiciously, but only one growled. Keeping his voice low and steady, he chatted away to them as he slowly placed the bowls on the floor, avoiding any sudden movements. "Here you go, grubs up." He crouched by the bowls to encourage the dogs and pushed them towards them. "I believe lamb with a few biscuits for texture is on the menu today. Yum, yum. It looks quite lovely. Come on. Seriously boys, I don't bite."

The dogs hesitantly shuffled forward with eyes full of mistrust.

"I dread to think what happened to you guys in the past, but it's all over now. Ted will come and feed you for the next couple of days. I'll do my best to make sure Chris is home quickly." He picked up the envelope with the wills and stepped back as the dogs suspiciously sniffed the food before tucking in.

"Mission accomplished," Simon said, backing towards the door. Outside, he rang Ted and persuaded the dog handlers they were no longer needed. Next, he handed the wills to an officer and explained how Chris said they came to be in his possession.

The unimpressed officer looked at him in disbelief and slipped the envelope inside an evidence bag. In a condescending voice, he said. "I need you to come to the station to make a statement about your fanciful beliefs."

"Good, because that was on the top of my to-do list," Simon

said.

"Actually," Peter said. "The first thing on your list is to call Kate. I've told her you're okay, but she expects a call from you."

Walking down the track to their cars, Peter said, "Do you really believe him?"

"Absolutely. Without a shadow of a doubt," Simon replied confidently.

"That's handy because you also believed Rob, who now has been released because we proved him to be innocent," Peter said, not attempting to keep his sarcasm from his voice.

"I'll bet my life Chris is innocent and is telling the truth."

"I think you just did that with the dogs," Peter said.

"We must have made a mistake about Rob somewhere along the line," Simon said. He went on to explain how the wills had turned up and why he believed Chris.

Peter went quiet, weighing up everything Simon said until they reached their cars. "If you're right, then we've missed something obvious that has been staring us in the face."

"What?"

"After you've given your statement, meet me back at the office. I need to check something."

CHAPTER FIFTY-NINE

Simon found Peter in the back room, looking at the footage from the traffic cameras. He gave the screen a cursory look before heading for the coffee machine. "Do you need a top-up? What they gave me at the station was disgusting. Despite everything I said, they seem to be intent on charging Chris. I feel so responsible. He shouldn't be in there."

Peter accepted a fresh cup of coffee and leaned back in his chair to look at Simon. "What happened back there to make you change your tune? You can't have told me everything."

Simon slumped into the chair next to Peter. "Chris is a jerk, I accept that. So am I, if I'm honest. But he didn't kill his sister. He cried real tears for her." Simon shrugged. "He's not a people person but his sister was the one person who understood him. I don't know what happened during their childhood, but it was something they shared - a bond that held them together. He disliked Rob because he was afraid of losing her. He wouldn't ever have done something to hurt her."

"I still think there's something more you're not telling me." Peter tapped the computer screen. "But I don't think he did."

Simon put down his mug and craned his neck to see the screen. "What am I looking at?"

"We should have put the pieces together as soon as we saw the will. Only one person had nothing to lose and everything to gain from Jane's death."

Simon frowned. "The money was to be split equally between Rob and Chris."

"And they were both happy to have her around," Peter said.

"One of the charities or ... you can't mean Lucy?" Simon started to pace the room. "Lucy? Are you serious?"

Peter called Simon over and tapped the screen again. "This is Lucy's car heading towards Jane's home. We know Rob called her from the park bench. He doesn't remember making the call, but as Jane had thrown him out, he probably made all sorts of criticisms. We also know what a daddy's girl she is."

Simon squinted at the screen. "Her boyfriend said she was with him all evening."

"So, he lied."

"Do you ever believe what people tell you?"

"Occasionally," Peter said. "I can't believe we overlooked this possibility before."

"Because she seemed a sweet girl, worried about her father," Simon said. "What do you think happened?"

"After receiving her father's call, Lucy drove to collect him. When she found the park bench empty, she went to the house and saw the wills on the side. Jane probably forgot to take them up with her when she went to bed. Without that oversight, she would still be alive."

"She may have left them out on purpose for Rob to see when he came home," Simon said.

"We'll never know, but until that moment, Lucy probably had no idea what a windfall was coming her way. But Jane could live another forty years, or as she had just thrown her father out, split up with him. Lucy saw the chance to get Jane out of her father's life and guarantee a tidy sum for herself."

"She had me fooled," Simon admitted. "Where's Lucy now?"

"I phoned Rob earlier to tell him Chris had been taken into custody. I had hoped to ask him a few questions, but Lucy answered the phone. Rob was busy carrying her stuff back up to her bedroom. I'm hoping Jake will feel used by her sudden dash back to Daddy and be prepared to tell us the truth about that night. I somehow doubt it was the first time he has taken second place to her father." Peter tapped the screen again. "The time on the footage confirms she jumped in her car straight after the call."

Simon leapt to his feet. "Okay, you've convinced me. What are we waiting for? We could have Chris out in a couple of hours."

"I don't know about you, but I'm going to finish my coffee."

CHAPTER SIXTY

Driving to Jake's home, Simon was surprisingly quiet. Peter took advantage of the peace and quiet for the first half of the journey. Finally, he said, "You're quiet."

"Thinking some things that Chris said over. Do you think I'm a spoilt idiot?"

"Not particularly."

"Do you think I'm reliable?"

"Sometimes," Peter said, not sounding sure.

Simon nodded and fell silent again.

"Is something bothering you?" Peter asked.

"No," Simon said. A short while later, he asked, "Do you think I'm wasting my life?"

"No more than anyone else."

"I'm going to change."

"In what way?"

"In every way."

Peter glanced across and gave Simon a hard stare. "What on earth did Chris say to you?"

"Nothing in particular, but he got me thinking about some things," Simon said. "How come you are so unaffected by people? And never believe anything anyone says? I believed Jake when he said he spent the night with Lucy. It would never have occurred to me he might have lied."

Peter sighed. "It's what twenty-plus years in the police does for you. I've spent far too much time seeing the worst side of people and the pain they leave behind."

"You've developed a natural feel for when people are lying?"

Peter laughed hollowly. "You were right the first time. My

default position is I don't believe anyone."

"So everyone is a suspect?"

"Potentially," Peter said. "People are capable of all sorts of things when their backs are against the wall, or they want something. Millions of smug, law-abiding people are innocently walking around only because their resolve has not yet been tested."

"That's a jaded view of humanity if ever I heard one."

"I don't disagree," Peter said.

"How do you live with that?"

"I manage."

Simon turned to watch the scenery flashing by. He wanted more from life than simply managing as the days slipped by. He wanted his life to mean something. Was that so unreasonable? "Are you hoping Jake will admit Lucy wasn't with him all night?" When Peter nodded, Simon asked, "Then what?"

"We'll persuade him to come with us to speak with DI Ford. Along with the footage of Lucy's car, I'm hoping he will arrest Lucy or at least take her in for questioning."

"And then what? Job done for us. Does it bother you that you won't be around for the arrest?"

"They've got their job to do, and I'll ask him to keep us updated so that if they arrest Lucy this evening, we'll know about it."

"It must still rub though, when you used to be the one in the thick of it all."

"Simon."

"Yes?"

"Shut up."

Peter was pleased to see Simon shrug and decide to scroll through his phone rather than keep talking. He wasn't going to admit he was going to feel deflated. He had enjoyed having the freedom to investigate how he thought best, but he would miss the satisfaction of the final arrest. He would watch the trial with interest as a bystander. He doubted he would be called as a witness. They had done most of the leg work, but the station wouldn't want to admit that. He could see DCI Harris somehow spinning it to suggest he suspected the daughter all along. He could claim he held Rob on remand in the hope that Lucy would confess.

He told himself he should be satisfied with a job well done, but it didn't help how he felt. He glanced over when Simon's phone pinged.

After checking, Simon said, "That's a bit awkward. Lucy has just settled our bill."

"That's how it's supposed to work," Peter said. "I'm surprised Charlie doesn't insist on some of the bill being paid upfront."

"You don't feel even the tiniest little bit guilty?"

"Why should I? She instructed us to prove her dad was innocent, and that's what we've done."

"You don't feel bad about taking her money when we're about to argue for her arrest?"

"No! She killed her dad's girlfriend because she saw the wills on the side and read them. When her dad was suspected, she tried to blame Jane's brother, even planting evidence. She probably sees our fee as a small price to pay out of the inheritance she thinks is coming her way."

"That's harsh."

"That's reality," Peter said. "If you're going to stick with this game, you need to get your head around the fact life isn't a fairy tale for most people. For many, it's a daily struggle and a miserable chore."

"Nothing like a cheery disposition to make the day go with a swing," Simon said. A short while later, he added, "I still feel uncomfortable about taking her money."

"Why? She asked us to investigate her father's guilt as she thought - or knew as we now know - he was innocent. We did that, and he's been released."

"I guess," Simon muttered. "Do you think Lucy is safe? Would Rob attack her if he worked out that she killed Jane?"

While considering the question Peter pulled the car to a halt outside Jake's house. "On the balance of probability, no."

"You don't think we should go and check?"

"We can't turn up there ahead of the police. She thinks Chris is in custody and she is home and dry. We won't be popular if we show up and she bolts."

Simon hadn't moved or undone his seatbelt. "We could pop in to congratulate Rob on his release."

Peter sighed. Popping around to check on them went against his better judgment, not least because Simon had expressed his conflicted views about accepting Lucy's fee. He hoped that once the police had taken Jake's statement and viewed the traffic camera footage, they would be on their way to make an arrest. But Simon had planted seeds of doubt in his mind. What if Rob remembered more about his late-night call to his daughter and asked her about it? How would either of them react if the truth came out? Rob had warned them how he would react if he discovered who killed Jane, but Lucy's reaction worried him more.

"Once we know she's okay, we can go on our merry way before the police arrive," Simon said. "If everything goes as you've planned, they'll still be talking Jake through his statement. We'll be leaving before they've even left the station."

"And you promise you'll do no more than shake Rob's hand and thank Lucy for her prompt payment of the bill?"

"Yes."

"And if it's offered, we won't go in for a celebratory drink."

Simon pulled a face. "We won't cross the threshold."

"And it goes on record that this was your idea. You told me it was your standard practice to pay a courtesy call on the completion of cases."

"Naturally."

"I'll think about it," Peter said, opening the car door. "Let's see what Jake has to say."

CHAPTER SIXTY-ONE

Jake opened the door with glazed eyes and alcohol on his breath. "Oh, it's you. Lucy isn't here. She's back with her father."

"It's you we came to see," Peter said over loud music coming from inside the house. "Can we come in?"

Jake opened the door wider and stepped back. "I don't see why not." He led them into an untidy living room where a dishevelled-looking guy about the same age as him was sitting on the floor looking through old LPs, surrounded by empty beer bottles.

"Can you turn the music down?" Peter asked.

Jake shrugged and lifted the needle on the spinning desk before plonking himself on the sofa. "Ask away."

"It's about the night Jane was murdered. You said Lucy was here all night. That wasn't true, was it?"

"Yes, it was," Jake said, ignoring his friend's snigger. "Why would I lie about it?"

"To protect your girlfriend."

"She was here like I said."

Jake's friend smirked and muttered something to himself. Simon turned to him and asked, "Have you something to say?"

"Yeah, shut up, Ray," Jake said.

Ray held his hands up in submission. "Hey, it's none of my business. I get it."

"You know it's an offence to lie to the police?" Peter asked.

"You're not the police," Jake said.

"No, but they'll be coming to see you once we show them evidence that Lucy wasn't with you all night like you said," Peter said. "Traffic cameras picked up her car travelling towards Jane's house a little before midnight. It would look better for you if you saved them a trip out here."

"She's not worth getting yourself into trouble, mate," Ray said. "Once the police start sniffing around, they'll never leave you alone."

Jake looked less sure of himself and asked, "What difference would it make? She had nothing to do with Jane's death."

"She left the house after receiving her father's call, didn't she?"

"Only briefly," Jake said. "Rob called, saying he was sleeping on a bench because he'd been kicked out. Luce went to find him and bring him here. When she couldn't find him, she came back. Telling you that would have only complicated things unnecessarily."

"That's what she told you to say?" Peter asked.

"It made sense."

"Did you see her when she arrived back?"

"I'd had a busy day."

"You were asleep and didn't see her until the following morning?"

"I can vaguely remember her crawling back into bed," Jake said. "I asked her if she had found him, and she said no."

"Do you remember what she was wearing that night?" Peter asked.

"Yeah, a dress she knows I like her wearing. It's black with moons and stars on it, and has those flared sleeves like in the seventies."

"Have you seen her wear it since?"

"No, but ..."

"Could you go upstairs and look for it?" Peter asked.

"No point," Jake said. "She's taken all her stuff."

"Would you mind if Simon went up to check?"

"I'll go with him," Ray said, getting up from the floor. "Make sure he doesn't poke around too much."

CHAPTER SIXTY-TWO

When Simon and Ray returned downstairs, Peter and Jake had moved to the kitchen and were drinking black coffee. Simon shook his head and leaned against the counter. Peter looked up and said, "When we've finished these, Jake is coming with us to the station to make a statement. I've called ahead, and DI Ford will be waiting for us."

Ray hesitantly said, "Umm … Can I have a quick word with Jake? In private?"

Peter frowned. He didn't want Ray to talk Jake out of making a statement, but he couldn't see how he could object. It was probably something irrelevant anyway about a stash of drugs that needed to be hidden before they left. "Is it something you can say in front of us? We're not the police, and we're not concerned with any other minor offences."

"Umm … it's private," Ray mumbled.

Peter drank his coffee, watching the two men disappear from the room with a sinking heart. They still had the footage of Lucy's car, but Jake's evidence would strengthen the case against Lucy.

Simon slid into the chair opposite. "What do you think that's about?"

"No idea. Did you see anything untoward upstairs? Any drugs or stolen property?"

"It was hard to see anything amongst the muddle up there," Simon admitted. "But what I didn't find were any feminine products - not so much as a hairbrush, let alone any clothes."

"Did you check at the bottom of the wardrobe and the laundry basket?"

"He hasn't got one, but yes, I looked through a pile of dirty clothes, under the bed and in the back of the wardrobe."

Jake returned looking ashen. "I think there's something you need to know. A while back, I found a handgun. I've been meaning to hand it into the police, honest. I just haven't got around to it with one thing and another. Work has been hectic. And, well, it's gone."

"Was it loaded?"

"Er ... I found some ... yeah. Everything's gone."

CHAPTER SIXTY-THREE

Peter jumped up from the table, taking charge. "Okay, Jake, go to the station as we agreed. Take Ray with you if you like. DI Ford might not be available, but there'll be someone who can take your statement. Simon, you can ring Ford from the car and explain the situation, and that we are on our way." With that, he sped out of the room. Simon rushed after him, pulling out his phone.

Peter pulled away from the pavement to a squeal of brakes and the honking of a horn. Simon held the door as Peter swerved in and out of the traffic while waiting for his call to be answered.

When the call finished, Peter asked, "What did he say?"

"On no account were we to go to the house."

"I thought he might," Peter said, still accelerating towards Jane's house. He swung the car into the driveway and was out on the driveway before Simon had the chance to release his seatbelt.

Every light in the house was on, and a stereo was blaring music, partially covering loud shouting. A couple of bemused neighbours wandered out into the lane to see what was happening. Running to the front door, Peter shouted, "Everyone, go back inside. There's a firearm inside."

Peter and Simon shouted for Rob and threw themselves against the front door, but it wasn't budging. Simon set himself up to take another run at it when Peter stopped him. "It'll be quicker to get inside by breaking a window."

Still shouting Rob's name, Peter picked up a stone from the front rockery and used it to smash the small window to the side of the front door.

Simon helped Peter pull away the broken glass. "I'm smaller than you. Give me a leg up, and I'll let you in the front door."

Peter cupped his hands, and with one heave, Simon was inside a small downstairs bathroom. The house was throbbing with the bass of a rock song. He quickly opened the door for Peter, and they started along the corridor. Voices were coming from the kitchen at the rear of the house, but they were quieter now and could only just be heard as a quiet murmur beneath the rock music. Simon looked to Peter for direction, who put his finger to his lips.

They reached the closed kitchen door, which was almost pulsating with the loud beat of the music. Peter turned the handle and slowly opened the door. The music was deafening as they peered inside. Rob was sitting at the kitchen table facing them but, with his head in his hands, didn't see them. Lucy had her back to them, erratically waving a gun around in Rob's general direction. The crescendo of the arguing appeared to be finished and replaced by Rob's resignation and Lucy's indecision.

Peter nodded to the stereo in the corner of the room as he edged closer to Lucy. When Simon reached the stereo, Peter lunged at Lucy, grabbing her arms from behind and tackling her to the ground. The gun went off, harmlessly, breaking a kitchen tile.

Peter snatched the gun from Lucy and handed it backwards to Simon, who had switched off the music and was coming over to help. Peter had Lucy pinned against the floor with her arms behind her back when they heard the sirens of the approaching police cars. He shouted to Simon, "Put the gun down safely in the hallway somewhere and let them in. You had better hold your hands above your head as they are probably armed." As Simon left, Peter looked up and asked Rob if he was okay.

Tears were streaming down Rob's face. "You should have let her shoot me. My life is over. What's left for me now?"

The anguish in Rob's face took Peter back. He had nothing to offer him, so he stayed quiet. He had occasionally doubted Rob's love for Jane but had never questioned his feelings about his daughter. Maybe in the future, Rob would come to terms with what his precious little girl had done and visit her in prison, but right now, it was clear he would rather be dead. Hadn't he felt that way not so long ago?

Peter turned away when the officers arrived to take charge of Lucy. There was nothing more for him to do, so he went to search for Simon, hoping he hadn't got himself arrested. He found him outside the house and wandered over. "Okay?"

"Yeah. You? Pint?"

"Not so fast, you two," DI Ford said, emerging from nowhere. He spent the next five minutes criticising their actions before he was called away.

Peter shrugged. "A pint sounds perfect, but won't Kate be expecting you home?"

"She'll understand. Anyway, I want to thank you."

"What for?"

"Putting up with me. I've enjoyed working with you." Simon hesitantly asked, "I hope I do again?"

"We'll see."

"And you're right. I did realise a few things when I was in the house with Chris, thinking I was going to die. I have a few issues to work out."

"Shouldn't you be telling Kate this?"

"Yes, but I could do with a sounding board first. Are you up for it?"

"I'm not sure what use I'll be, but come on partner," Peter said, patting him on the back and leading the way to his car.

CHAPTER SIXTY-FOUR

Simon didn't say another word until he was halfway through his pint, and Peter didn't know how to prompt him. He knew how to question witnesses and apply pressure on suspects to get to the truth, but he had no idea how to ask another person about their innermost feelings. He didn't even know how to express his own and began to doubt he could help. He wished he was more of a sports fan so he could talk about football or rugby, cricket even. The last television he watched was some bland rubbish on Netflix, which Simon had probably never heard of, and the last album he listened to, *The Trick of the Tail* by Genesis was released before Simon was even born. After staring into his glass for inspiration, he finally found the courage to ask, "What is it you want to talk about?"

Simon shrugged. "You were probably right. I should be having this conversation with Kate."

With a combination of relief and a sense of failure, Peter said, "Women are better at these things, aren't they? But if you ever want a male perspective, I might be able to help."

Simon looked down for a long time. He looked up and mumbled, "I feel a bit of a tool, but I think I need professional help."

"Okay," Peter said slowly, taken aback by Simon's honesty. "Why's that?"

"I don't think I've accepted the death of my family. I mean, of course, I know they're dead. I'm not stupid. It's just ... I don't have the words for how I feel."

Peter's mind shot to his parents. They had given him a happy childhood, but as an adult, he had moved away and not kept in contact as much as he should have. He had regretted that when they died. The sudden finality of death and the realisation he couldn't go back and make amends hit hard, but by then, he had a daughter to take care of, and he consoled himself with the thought they had lived a long life. It was hardly the same.

He didn't want to acknowledge how he had fallen apart when his first wife died. The raw pain and guilt were something he didn't want to remember. He had handled it badly, barely keeping his head above water for his daughter's sake. He couldn't advise anyone about the horrors of grief and loss. He hadn't even coped well when his last girlfriend decided to return to France.

"I guess we should go," Simon said, although he didn't move from his seat.

"Grief is complicated," Peter said, preparing to leave. "It's not just sadness and loss. It's anger, guilt, confusion and regret all tangled up together. It doesn't make sense, and it doesn't go away."

"I wish it would," Simon said. "Sometimes it doesn't feel as though I'm living. It's like I'm already half-dead. I died with them. Everything is fuzzy, and there's a barrier between me and real living. I can't move on until I somehow break through the barrier. That's what I need help with. How to break through."

"If I could tell you how to do that, I would." Peter gave a wry smile. "If you work out how to do it, come back and tell me."

"I will. And thanks, I appreciate it."

"I'm not sure what you're thanking me for, but I'll take it."

"For not judging and making me feel like a weak failure and less of a man. For admitting you've felt something similar. I think I've already made a breakthrough by starting the conversation with you. I'm ready to talk things through with Kate, and I'll make an appointment with someone tomorrow." Simon pushed back from the table. "Let's go."

During the drive to Holly Bush Farm, their conversation returned to the safety of superficiality. Before pulling into the driveway, Peter asked, "I think you've made the right decision, but what was it Chris said to you that pushed you in the right direction?"

"Poor Chris. I had almost forgotten about him. I hope they release him tonight so he can get home to his dogs," Simon said. "It wasn't anything he said. He isn't a bad person, but I saw how his hurt had led him to where he is. When I thought I might die, I realised I wanted to live, but not like this."

"Concentrate on your conversation with Kate. I'll call the station when I get home to check on Chris," Peter said. "And if you ever want to talk, you've got my number. Give me a call, and we can meet up any time."

"Thanks. I would like that." Simon stepped out of the car and looked up at the farmhouse. The house held so many memories for him, good and bad, and he resolved to himself that he was going to sort himself out and make more good ones. He poked his head back into the car. "Wish me luck."

"You don't need any. You've got this," Peter said.

Simon saw the hallway light go on as Peter's car pulled away. He hadn't said much to Peter, but he already felt less weight on his shoulders. Moving towards the doorway, he thought Peter was right. He had this. He had taken the all-important first steps of accepting he had a problem and couldn't solve it all alone.

Thank you so much for reading my book. I hope you enjoyed reading it as much as I enjoyed writing it.

I always enjoy seeing what people think of my books so if you have the time a quick review or a rating would be brilliant.

If you would like to know a little more about me and my books please say hello on my Facebook page.
Facebook.com/61560769589326

BOOKS IN THIS SERIES

Chapman and Morris Mystery

Trouble At Clenchers Mill

A Charming English village mystery. When a neighbour is accused of attempting to kill her ex-husband, Simon Morris jumps at the chance to practice his sleuthing skills and prove her innocence. His amateur investigations draw him into the murky world of village politics and on-line predators as he uncovers a collective effort to drive Richard Fielding and his new family out of Clenchers Mill. And behind the smokescreen of unpleasant bullying, there is one person who is determined to see Richard dead. Without some quick thinking and the help of his dogs, Simon's first case may prove to be the death of them all.

Trouble At Fatting House

A charming English village mystery.A stand-alone Chapman and Morris Mystery.Simon and Kate land the perfect house-sitting job in a quirky, old farmhouse.But, when the neighbours are murdered, they discover the house has a sinister past connected to an identical killing.Following another attack, Simon disappears, and the police uncover disturbing secrets about his past.Compelling evidence against Simon mounts, leaving Kate alone, unsure what to believe or who to trust. Is Simon the killer? Or a pawn in somebody else's game?As Kate closes in on the truth, she realises too late that the stakes are far higher than she ever imagined.

Trouble At Suncliffe Manor

A charming English village mystery.A stand-alone Chapman and Morris Mystery.After a tough winter, Kate is excited to receive a new house-sitting job in a clifftop manor house. As soon as they arrive, she experiences feelings of insecurity and the increasing sense she is being watched. Her sense of vulnerability is escalated by the paranoia of a young groom who does little to hide her attraction to Simon while persuading him to investigate the death of her grandmother. She believes her relative was murdered after seeing someone whose funeral she attended years earlier.While Simon chases ghosts in the shadows a very real threat is looming ever closer.

Trouble At Sharcott

Appearances can be deceptive.

A charming English village mystery.

Simon is asked to protect the eldest daughter of a local property developer during a family celebration. The family have received a series of disturbing threats, but the developer doesn't want to involve the police. The celebration goes well, but Simon makes a decision with fatal consequences.
When the younger daughter asks for his help, there are many reasons why he should stay away from the family. But Simon wants to redeem himself. A friend's future depends on him getting it right this time. But will he?